Belene Island

Geoff Hart

Belene Island

Geoff Hart

Prologue

Tsvetan's heart was pumping. His feet were in tatters and bleeding badly. His head ached.

"Keep going; just keep going!" he told himself again and again, but his body was getting to the point where it could no longer obey his commands. He could hear them behind him, not far now. If he did not reach the shore in the next few minutes they would be on him. He just hoped to God that Milen would be there. He had promised. When had he ever promised and failed to deliver? Never! He would surely not let him down now.

The prison wardens from the Belene Labour Camp had only limited experience of pursuing prisoners across this part of the island. Since the camp opened in 1949 only four inmates had breached the perimeter of the labour camp and none of those had made it this far.

Tsvetan had expected to surprise everyone. He was a model prisoner who appeared to accept the punishments and hardships handed down to him without complaint. Surely no one had for a moment expected him to try to escape. He had anticipated gaining some advantage from the element of surprise. He had also thought to further confound the guards by heading not for the shores of Bulgaria's mainland but towards Romania. The prison population was exclusively Bulgarian and most inmates would have regarded flight to Romania as more dangerous than staying put. Tsvetan had anticipated that by the time the guards had organised their pursuit of him he would already be half way to the shore. However, to his dismay they seemed to know his intended route and were now no more than four hundred metres behind him.

Tsvetan could see light ahead of him indicating that he was on the edge of the forest. With a renewed energy he thrust forward and burst out of the forest onto the gravelly shore, squinting against the sudden onslaught of light. The small pebbles were hard beneath his bare feet, but he hardly noticed the pain. He looked up and with relief saw Milen's thirty year old boat.

Despite the situation his mind was suddenly filled with memories of himself and Milen as young men fishing on the banks of the Danube in this very boat. It was a wonderful memory of life before communist occupation; a memory of another time. Tsvetan's eyes scanned the shoreline desperately, searching for his friend. Then he saw him. Fifty metres from the boat Milen's apparently lifeless body lay on the ground while the tide lapped around him. With the guards almost upon him Tsvetan was faced with an agonising decision: should he run to Milen to see if there was any life left in him or to the possible safety of the boat?

Chapter One

For the third time Tsvetan reeled in and recast his line. Despite the perfect conditions he was finding it difficult to concentrate.

"It's bloody awful, Milen. The Nazi Party are going to take the whole of Europe into war and our pathetic government looks like siding with them. And what does the Orthodox Church do? They do nothing and say nothing. It all makes me so angry!"

Milen did not want to get into this conversation, not on such a lovely day. The weather was warm and the river was still. A swarm of black flies lit up by the rays of the sun were dancing on the surface of the water. It was a wonderful day for fishing. "Don't worry so, Tsvetan. Just enjoy the day. One thing is certain, there is nothing we can do about it."

Although not yet eighteen years old Tsvetan was a young man with strong opinions. He would not be so easily deterred from his subject. "The Nazis are ruthless savages, but our government seem to think what they do is acceptable. I am a patriotic Bulgarian, but if Bulgaria takes Germany's side I am damned if I will remain loyal."

Milen could see the prospect of a pleasant day's fishing rapidly retreating.

Tsvetan continued. "Don't get me wrong, Milen. I love our life here in Svishtov. It would be wonderful if our only concerns were fishing on the Danube and watching girls, but unlike you I can't just forget about all the bad things going on around us."

"If you found yourself in bed with Tatyana you would soon stop worrying about all the evil in the world," said Milen. "That girl could make a boy forget his own name. She really has her eye on you. Why don't you try it on with her? Believe me, that's what she wants."

"Don't be so crude, Milen," retorted Tsvetan. "I have known her since kindergarten. I don't think of her like that," he said, not altogether truthfully.

"Look, friend, we are nearly eighteen and neither of us has been with a girl yet. It is about time we got started. If she's willing, why not?"

Tsvetan smiled at his friend who for all his talk was terrified of girls. He put his arm around Milen's shoulder.

7

"Stop thinking about Tatyana. I think we both need to concentrate on the fishing. We haven't caught anything yet. I think our wild talk is frightening the fish away. At this rate we won't have anything for supper tonight."

Milen turned to pay some attention to his fishing rod. "It's this confounded boat," he maintained. "My father never caught anything in it and we hardly fare any better. It is an unlucky vessel." Just at that moment there was a tug on Milen's line and all thoughts of Tatyana disappeared. He was hungry and he wanted that fish.

Milen reeled the fish in and expertly landed it in the boat at Tsvetan's feet. "It's a beauty!" Tsvetan exclaimed. "See, fishing has its moments too. It is more rewarding and less confusing than chasing girls. Bulgarian women are certainly beautiful. For now I am happy just to look at them."

"There's something wrong with you, my friend," Milen told him. "Next time I go fishing I will take Nicholai or Dido with me so I can have a normal conversation. You are so solemn."

"There is much to be solemn about, Milen," replied Tsvetan.

Seeing that faraway look on his friend's face, Milen fell silent and kept his fantasies about the beautiful local girls of Svishtov to himself while Tsvetan went back to worrying about things that, as far as Milen was concerned, belonged to another world.

The two friends stayed another couple of hours on the water and despite what Milen had said about the boat being unlucky they had an excellent catch between them. With some fresh vegetables from the garden to accompany the fish both families would eat well that night. As they walked home with their catch in the warmth of the late evening sunshine Tsvetan felt happy in spite of himself. True there were many events at home and abroad to vex him, but life as a young man growing up by the beautiful banks of the Danube was to be enjoyed. Milen was certainly right about that.

"What are you smiling about?" asked Milen. "Thinking about Tatyana, after all?"

"I wasn't, no," replied Tsvetan, "Although I have to admit that conjuring up visions of her does bring some pleasure with it."

"Yes and getting her into bed would bring considerably more pleasure, I am sure," said Milen, reducing his friend's thoughts to something he better understood.

"I will keep your advice in mind," retorted Tsvetan and the two walked the rest of the way home in a contented silence.

The two young men were well known in the small town of Svishtov and those who knew them held both boys in high regard.

They were so rarely seen apart that most people thought of Milen and Tsvetan as two halves of a whole. If asked for an opinion on one of them most people would automatically express a view on the other one too. If seeking Milen people would generally ask, "Have you seen Milen and Tsvetan?" and vice versa. The expectation was always that they would be together and more often than not they were. Despite all of this they were quite different young men in appearance as well as in personality.

Milen was strongly built, like a hundred metres runner. He held himself erect, as the proud Bulgarian he was. He had an honest well-proportioned face. When he laughed, as he did often, his brown eyes sparkled in a way that suggested mischief and usually this impression was not misleading. Tsvetan was more slightly built, much smaller than his friend, with slim wrists and slender hands almost like a girl's. His light coloured hair and green eyes set him apart from the crowd and gave him an almost alien quality. His body was slim and he moved with a graceful ease. Unlike his friend, getting Tsvetan to smile let alone laugh was no easy undertaking, but well worth the effort.

Tsvetan and Milen had both been born and raised in Svishtov. They had attended the same schools and had the same group of friends. Their families lived in the same street and they had spent their childhood in and out of each other's houses. They were both proud of their town and Milen at least had no plans to live or even travel far beyond its boundaries. Svishtov was a culturally rich town with a history dating back to Roman times. It was a particular source of pride to Tsvetan that the town had been a centre in the political struggles for national liberation, and the birthplace of key writers and intellectuals.

Its most famous son, Dimitar Apostolov Tsenov had been a large-scale entrepreneur and merchant, an ardent patriot and an advocate of cultural and educational development. He had bequeathed his fortune to the citizens of Svishtov, to build an economic institute in the town. The Academy bearing his name had opened just a few years earlier and both boys were expected to attend. Their parents, although humble fisher folk, had high hopes for their eldest sons and were determined that they should take advantage of the new opportunity for higher education in the town. Milen's father was a member of the fledgling Communist Party of Bulgaria and was adamant that his son was entitled to the same level of education as the young men from wealthier families.

Proud as he was of his home town with its new university,

Tsvetan had ambitions to travel and to see something of the world and if he was going to attend university he would at the very least want to study in Sofia or Varna. His friend Milen was aware of this ambition, but so far Tsvetan had not found the courage to speak of it to his parents. Anyway, this was at least a year off and all he could do at present was concentrate on his school work and help support his family through fishing and aiding his father on the family smallholding. Thoughts about the old universities he might attend and the beautiful Bulgarian girls he might meet in the big cities would have to wait.

Tatyana was only just seventeen, but she was already old enough to know what she wanted from life. She had inherited this trait from her mother, Yordana, a fiercely independent and self-confident woman who was somewhat out of place in the female community of Svishtov. Tatyana's mother had also known who she wanted as a husband and had relentlessly pursued Tatyana's father until he eventually submitted to her considerable charms and married her. Tatyana was also similar to her mother in this respect; she too knew who she wanted as a partner. Milen had not been wrong regarding her feelings towards Tsvetan, although he expressed the sentiment with a crudity that did not really match Tatyana's romantic notions. She thought about him constantly and in her mind's eye she imagined herself by his side, attentive to his every need; lovers and companions for life.

However, in one respect she was very different to her assertive mother. Although she tried to target her affections on Tsvetan, in his company she became ridiculously tongue-tied, unable to say anything beyond the most banal. She was aware that Tsvetan was interested in a girl's mind and personality as much as her appearance and she liked to think of herself as a serious person who thought deeply about the world. Yet whenever the opportunity arose to show this side of herself she instead behaved like an imbecile who had nothing to say on any subject. Tatyana despaired of her inability to behave normally around him and yet she could see that in spite of everything Tsvetan did seem to like her. She had no idea why. Perhaps he just felt sorry for her which would be unbearable or maybe, even worse, he simply regarded her as a nice young girl, someone he had known all his life that he cared about.

Tatyana was a pretty girl, but no more so than many of her friends and contemporaries. She understood this, but was not at all aware that, young as she was, she had that indefinable something that made men notice her. She had a feline quality about her and it was her languid manner and movement that caught the male eye. She was as sultry as the summer heat and just as intoxicating. She had no reason to worry about the target of her affections. There was no doubt that Tsvetan was paying attention.

Chapter Two

Tsvetan was an avid reader of newspapers and it was from these that he got most of his information as well as many of his opinions about world events. His father was a simple man who could barely read and had a deep rooted suspicion about newspapers which he believed dealt mainly in lies. His mother came from a different sort of family where books and periodicals were commonplace and she spent much of her limited relaxation time with her head in a novel or indeed any book that she could get her hands on. However, she never managed to persuade her husband to lift his ban on newspapers even when Tsvetan developed an interest in reading them. Unable to read at home Tsvetan found his own solution and at least twice a week he would remain at school after lessons and read his teacher's newspaper. The old schoolmaster, Slavko Nikolov, was only too willing to encourage this interest. He was aware that Tsvetan was an exceptional student and was more than happy to facilitate his quest for knowledge. The school teacher and his young pupil spent many happy hours together discussing politics, religion and current affairs in both Bulgaria and Europe.

Nikolov became a major influence on the young man's early development, for although Tsvetan did discuss such things with his mother she was not well informed about the modern world. It was Nikolov who first caused him to question the traditions of the Orthodox Church, although this was not an outcome that his teacher had particularly sought. He had simply informed Tsvetan about all the work that the Catholic Church had been involved in within Bulgaria: opening schools, colleges, and hospitals throughout the country, and offering scholarships to students who wished to study abroad. Like all his friends and family, Tsvetan had been brought up within the Orthodox Church and he was a devout Christian. However, he had long since believed that the church should be interested in the general welfare of its parishioners not just their spiritual wellbeing and was impressed by the Catholic Church's involvement in practical matters such as education and healthcare.

*

Tsvetan was out on the Danube again fishing with his friend Milen. Despite his threats to the contrary Milen had not invited either Dido or Nicholai to join him instead.

"Why would I go fishing with them?" he asked rhetorically. "With you I am guaranteed laughter even if it is just me making fun of you. Anyway you are a skilled fisherman. I am sure our two friends are good at something, but so far no one has discovered what it is!"

Tsvetan laughed. "I am sure that is unfair, Milen. I would hate to hear what you say about me."

"Then you shall hear it," his friend replied. "I tell people you are a pain in the bum; that you are too serious for your own good; that you are screwed up over your feelings for Tatyana, but that otherwise you are the best friend a man could have."

Uncharacteristically Tsvetan blushed. "You know me well, Milen. I try to be a good friend, but I am sure that I often fall short and, yes, I am screwed up over my feelings for Tatyana. As to the rest of the description, I forgive you."

After a pause of several minutes it was Milen who broke the silence. "So I was right, you are in love with Tatyana?"

"I don't know if it is love," said Tsvetan. "I certainly think about her a lot and my thoughts aren't always very honourable."

"I am sure she would be relieved to hear it!" retorted Milen with a wicked smile.

This time Tsvetan seemed unable or unwilling to respond to his friend's remarks in the way Milen had intended and he carried on in a serious vein.

"It would be only too easy to settle down here, ask for Tatyana's hand and follow my father and grandfather by becoming a fisherman. I am sure my little brother will follow this course, but I want more. I don't just want to live a happy life. I want to make a difference in some way, to serve God."

For once Milen remained serious and gave some proper thought to what Tsvetan had said. "As long as I can remember, Tsvetan, you have been continuously grappling for some higher meaning in your life. I am not like you so I will resist the temptation to tell you what I would do. Settling down in this beautiful little town with a girl you love sounds idyllic to most people, but you are not like most people. If you must, go and find yourself, travel if you need to. Don't worry, friend, I will still be here when you return and if you are lucky Tatyana will be too."

Tsvetan looked at his friend with real affection. Slowly and silently they each returned to their own thoughts and to their fishing.

*

Slavko Nikolov made his way home from school, later than usual as he had been enjoying a very interesting conversation with his young pupil, Tsvetan. Slavko had always enjoyed teaching. He regarded it as an honour to be allowed to coach and develop young minds. Every so often a student came along who had a particularly strong desire to learn and Tsvetan was one such as he had rarely encountered before. His outlook on life was so mature given his age and his interests were extremely broad. He sucked in new information like a sponge, but also gave careful thought to what he had learned. As a teacher, Slavko found this most rewarding and he had developed a strong respect for the rather earnest young man. Today, following a report in the newspaper regarding the tension between new political thought and the church, they had discussed whether the church should concern itself with politics. Tsvetan had expressed some interesting and contemporary opinions on the matter.

Slavko Nikolov walked along the unremarkable street where he had lived since first coming to Svishtov as a young newly qualified teacher. Although there was a footpath alongside he walked in the road because the cobbled pavement had been virtually destroyed over the years by the roots of the many trees that lined the street. His wife, Vesela, had been gone nearly ten years, but in spite of this he still approached the house with some hope and expectation that she would be there. It was absurd, of course, but much as the disappointment caused him pain he was not yet ready to give up longing for her return. Vesela, had been a keen gardener producing all the vegetables that they needed as well as plums and grapes from which, with the help of his neighbour, he had produced excellent rakia. Now Slavko bought his vegetables from the market and his rakia from next door. His garden was a wilderness which he had not touched since the day Vesela left.

The circumstances of her disappearance remained a mystery. All her belongings including even her handbag and purse were left behind. Her clothes still hung in the old wardrobe that Slavko had built for her when they were first married. Convinced that she had been abducted Slavko had immediately notified her as a missing person to the police. The police appeared to do nothing for a few days and then suddenly they descended on him as the chief suspect in the case. Slavko spent two nights in custody in a police cell under intense interrogation. The questions they had asked him were ridiculous. When they got nowhere with this line of enquiry they released him and just stopped looking for his wife altogether. Since then they had shown no interest in her possible whereabouts. Any attempts by Slavko to reopen the enquiry were met with derision.

"She got fed up with you and left, Nikolov." The police inspector had told him. "Women are like that. She probably found someone younger or, even more likely, richer. Just forget her." But he could not forget her. He did not want to and never would.

On the way home Slavko had been trying to decide what to eat that evening. Although he had been alone for such a long time he still had not developed any skill at cooking and more often than not he just threw a few vegetables into a pan and then ate them with a piece of bread. Sometimes he just had something cold. For himself he was not bothered, but his young student Tsvetan had been worrying about him getting thinner and more frail. Last week he had even invited him back to his house for dinner.

"My mother is a wonderful cook," Tsvetan had asserted, "And she so longs for intelligent company. She would love you to come."

Slavko had been touched by the young boy's concern, but had of course declined the invitation. "I am a very good cook myself." Slavko had maintained. "You have no reason to worry about me." However he knew that Tsvetan would worry and he owed it to him to take better care of himself.

Slavko entered the dingy and unkempt house and immediately went to the larder to see what he had there that could be turned into a decent meal. All he found was a packet of dried lentils, two or three jars of pickled cucumbers and some black bread that was at least three days old.

"Even Tsvetan's mother would be hard pushed to make something of that," he mused. Suddenly it occurred to him that he had not eaten any meat for weeks. There and then he decided he would eat at the little bar at the end of the next street. Why not? His salary as a teacher was very modest, but given how little he spent on himself he could easily afford such a luxury from time to time. Slavko replaced his hat and left the house with a spring in his step. He was going to have fried chicken and he could taste it already.

Chapter Three

Tsvetan had been working all day in one of his family's fields just outside Svishtov. It was a beautiful location on the slope of the small ridge that overlooked the town. In the opposite direction he could just make out the old monastery known as the Shroud of the Holy Mother. Despite the pleasant surroundings he had spent the last six hours doing a job that he hated. In fact, harvesting the new asparagus shoots was a job that everyone disliked. Tsvetan never wore gloves when working in the fields, but in this case he had paid a hard price for doing the job without. Each spear had to be cut about three centimetres below the soil level and by the end of the day his hands were bleeding from brushing across the dry earth. At least the mindless job gave him time to think and for some time he had been reflecting on his conversation with Milen. He was now clear that there were two things that he urgently needed to address.

Firstly, he needed to tell his parents about his reluctance to study in his home town. He had lived in Svishtov all his life and wanted the opportunity to see what else the world had to offer. He longed to travel. Secondly he must somehow get his feelings straight regarding Tatyana. This was difficult enough, but the inevitable corollary of that was that he should speak to her about how he felt. He was clueless about how he should do this. Trying to be honest with himself he admitted inwardly that the prospect terrified him. Every young man in the village admired Tatyana. Why should she pay any particular attention to him and how he felt? Having said that he was reminded of Milen's assertion that Tatyana was keen on him. Tsvetan lacked the confidence to believe this for himself, but was aware that his friend's judgement on most things was more reliable than his own. Perhaps he did have a chance.

All his life Tsvetan had never kept anything from his parents, particularly not from his mother. He knew that Milen, the only person that was aware of his ambitions, would never say anything to them. Nevertheless he felt uncomfortable with the knowledge that they assumed he would study at the new economic institute in the town, whereas he himself had no such plan. On one level he knew that his desire to study in a large city, or even abroad was a selfish notion. His parents were not rich people, but despite this he was aware that they would make whatever sacrifices were needed to allow him to gain a good education. However, financing him to live and study elsewhere would put an intolerable burden on them, not only because of the added cost, but also because he would no longer be around to help his father with the work from which the family lived. In spite of this he was determined to study somewhere else and would suffer any level of hardship himself to make this possible. If he was faced with either studying in Svishtov or not at all he would take the latter course and make his way in the world by some means or another.

As Tsvetan threw the last of the asparagus spears into the cart he found the resolve he needed. He was confident in respect of the matter between him and his parents, but he knew that if he did not speak to Tatyana that very day his courage would fail him. He would get the crops home, clean himself up and head off to her parents' house where he was sure to find her. With the renewed energy that comes from firm intention he set off pulling the handcart at a brisk pace.

By the time he set off for Tatyana's house it was already past eight in the evening, but at least that meant that the family meal would already have concluded. If he was lucky, he thought to himself, he would find the lovely Tatyana sitting in the garden. It was one of the few gardens in the town that was dominated by lawns and flower beds rather than by fruit and vegetables and the Kovachev family was possibly the only one that used their garden as a place for recreation and relaxation. The large number of trees and bushes that had been retained in the garden meant the place was alive with birdsong.

Tsvetan was lucky and to his relief he saw that she was sitting on her own, not together with her formidable mother as he had feared. As he approached Tatyana looked round and he could see at once that she had been crying. Her eyes were puffy and slightly bloodshot. In spite of her efforts to stop it, her shoulders still moved up and down to silent sobs. For all this she still had the power to captivate him with one look.

"Tsvetan, it is you! I had not expected you. Is everything alright?" Tatyana was flustered by his sudden appearance and hurriedly tried to wipe the tears from her face. She looked up at him anxiously, hoping that he had not noticed the state she was in, but it was too late.

"You have been crying, Tatyana. What is the matter? Is someone in the family unwell?"

Tsvetan's manner was one of genuine concern. He looked at her closely as if trying to read her thoughts. She returned his gaze trying to compose herself, but it was a mistake. His solemn, worried expression cut deep into her and her lip started to quiver, eventually giving way to a sharp intake of breath. Putting her two hands to her eyes and lowering her head she began to sob again. Now, now was the time. He should put his arm round her, hold her to him. He could see this was what she wanted, but he froze. Instead he just stared helplessly at her, rooted to the spot.

"What has happened to so upset you? Can I help in some way?"

Slowly Tatyana got a grip on her feelings to the point where she thought she could answer him without again bursting into tears.

"It is my mother. She has told father that she can no longer stand to live in a small town. We are moving away. She is so high and mighty. I was born here. I don't want to leave, but that does not concern her. We are going and that is that." Tatyana stood up and walked away a few paces keeping her back to Tsvetan. She thought she was going to cry again.

"Where are you going?" he called after her.

Misunderstanding him she replied, "Nowhere, I just wanted to walk about a bit. I am so angry with her." The change from being upset to angry dried her tears and she could turn to look at him again.

"No, I mean where are you moving to?"

"To Plovdiv. It is where my mother is from. All her family still live there. Apparently they can help my father find work. As for me, my mother says the schools there are excellent and I will be with like-minded girls, whatever that means." There was bitterness in her words.

Tsvetan was paralysed with grief and the lack of knowing how to respond. He had come here to tell her how he felt about her and now she was leaving. What could he do? He felt powerless. He spluttered out a reply that did nothing to express how he felt and did even less to satisfy what she had hoped to hear from him.

"I can understand that your mother wants to be near her family. You will be missed, all of you."

His response broke her heart. Was there no hope for her with him? She looked directly into his eyes. "Will you miss me, Tsvetan?" she asked.

Unable to hold her gaze, he sidestepped the question. "All your friends will miss you. You must know that."

For Tatyana his answer was like a dagger through her heart and for him represented a final defeat. He had let her go in order to spare her the difficulty of knowing his feelings whilst remaining hopelessly oblivious to hers. Without another word she turned and walked into the house, leaving him to his own thoughts, standing there in the garden like the fool he was.

The next day after school Tsvetan was sitting reading his teacher's newspaper while Slavko Nikolov was marking some exercise books. Tsvetan's mind was not really on the news story in front of him and he found himself returning to the start of the article again and again unable to take in what he was reading. When his teacher momentarily looked up from his task Tsvetan decided to ask him about the city which Tatyana's family were moving to.

"Excuse me, sir. Do you know the city of Plovdiv?"

The old teacher's mind was still focused on his marking so he took a little time to answer. "Plovdiv, you say. Yes, I know Plovdiv well. Why do you ask?"

Tsvetan tried to act nonchalant, detached from any interest in his own question. "No real reason. It is just that it is our second biggest city and I have never been there."

Slavko Nikolov was old, but he was not stupid and he was certainly not blind. He had noticed on enough occasions the chemistry between Tsvetan and Tatyana and he had also heard the rumours that the family were moving away, reportedly to Plovdiv. However, he gave nothing away and addressed the question in a detached way that was consistent with the manner in which the question had been asked.

"It is a beautiful and ancient city," he replied, "Well worth a visit. A place of high culture. It is particularly famous for the Roman ruins to be found there. I say ruins, but some of the ancient structures are in surprisingly good condition. Is there something in particular that interests you about the place?"

"Not really. It is just that I seem to know so little about our larger cities." Tsvetan replied unaware that his teacher could see right through him.

Slavko continued in the same vein. "During this century Plovdiv has also grown as an industrial and commercial centre. It has a particularly well developed food and tobacco industry as well as being of importance for modern trade and banking. All in all a place of real significance."

Tsvetan smiled. "You sound like a tourist guide," he observed.

The old teacher was more than a match for him. "Well, that is because you asked the question like a tourist."

*

A week had passed since Tsvetan's visit to Tatyana and he was still hurting from the news that she was to leave Svishtov. He had seen Tatyana a few times since then, but other than a rather frosty greeting she had not spoken to him. At first he found this baffling, but it was always in a public place that he had encountered her, in the school hall or on the street, and he concluded that her leaving was not widely known. That, he thought, might explain her reluctance to talk to him about it with others listening in. In any event he regarded her as lost to him and was determined to get on with his life without her, painful as this might be.

Unlike most young men Tsvetan did not immediately start thinking about other possible conquests. It was Tatyana that he had set his sights on and now that the possibility of her was gone he started to think of his life without the privilege of a female companion. Tsvetan's discussions with Slavko Nikolov about religion and in particular with regard to the Catholic Church continued. Slavko was becoming rather alarmed at the haste with which his young protégé was apparently closing in on a career within the church, particularly as he seemed to favour a life as a catholic priest with all the particular sacrifices that this path required. Tsvetan was young and impressionable, but even so the speed with which he seemed to have progressed from a general desire to study abroad to the notion of being a priest was a concern. Slavko worried that he had unwittingly contributed to this.

Given what he believed about Tsvetan's feelings towards Tatyana, Slavko found the idea of the young man opting for a celibate life worrying in the extreme. Slavko could not make up his mind whether it was appropriate to raise his anxieties with the young man. Indeed he sometimes worried that his notion that there was something between them was incorrect. He finally decided not to poke his nose in where it was not wanted unless Tsvetan directly sought his advice on the subject. After all he may be completely wrong about the part played by Tatyana's leaving in Tsvetan's consideration of the priesthood. For the time being at least he would remain silent.

*

Tatyana's mother, Yordana, could not wait to leave the little town of Svishtov behind her. A new life in her old city was beckoning and as the proposed date for their removal got closer she could speak of little else. She had known all along that her husband would not share her excitement. He was after all born and bred in the small town on the banks of the Danube and had no wish to leave it. He was doing it for her. She knew this and just hoped that once he had tasted all that city life had to offer he would settle and be happy in Plovdiv.

"It's where people go on holiday, not to live." had been his first reaction, but now he was resigned to it and would not do or say anything that may spoil his wife's anticipation of the move. This was the man she had married. He revered Yordana like a princess and she loved him in return.

With regard to her daughter's ridiculous attitude to the move Yordana showed considerably less patience and understanding. She was just about fed up with her daughter moping about the house as if the weight of the world were upon her. There and then she decided it was time to give her daughter a piece of her mind. She strode off towards the garden where she had last seen Tatyana. As expected she was sitting with her head in a book and a sullen expression on her face.

"Tatyana, what is it with you? Most girls of your age would be desperate to get out of this bourgeois little town, but you go around looking as if the world were about to end. What has got into you?"

"It might be a wretched little place to you, mother, but I like it here. I have friends here," retorted Tatyana. "There is nothing in Plovdiv for me. I don't know anyone except Nana and my aunts. I want to stay here. I can live with Uncle Kalin and his family."

"Don't be ridiculous, Tanya. How long would you last there? You couldn't sit in the garden reading all day. For a start you wouldn't find anything to read." Yordana could feel herself getting emotional and losing her temper at the same time. Her daughter's suggestion had hurt her.

Tatyana's face was flushed. She too could feel her anger rising. "They are good people. Don't speak of them in that way. It is Papa's family we are talking about."

Yordana tried to calm down. She loved her husband's brother and his family and was sorry for what she had said. "Of course they are good people," she admitted. "It is just that you upset me by suggesting you would stay behind. I have high hopes for both of us in Plovdiv. I know you will love it there."

Tatyana looked up at her mother whom, despite their differences, she greatly admired. She tried desperately to hold back the tears that were filling her eyes. She picked up her book and immediately put it down again. The tears were flowing now, beyond her control.

"It is Tsvetan," she announced through the tears. "I am in love with him."

Her mother took a step back. Her mouth hung open. In such a situation there is one thing that a mother must avoid saying. Yordana walked straight into it. "In love with Tsvetan? You can't be. You are only just seventeen, Tatyana. You are still a child."

"I *am* in love with him. I don't know why myself. When he is around me I can't think straight. It is as if he has cast a spell on me."

"You are being ridiculous, Tanya. You have no idea what love is."

Tatyana grabbed the serviette that she had been using as a book marker, rose suddenly from the chair and ran into the house, mopping her eyes.

"Tanya, don't run off!" her mother called after her, but her daughter paid no heed.

*

Eventually, almost inevitably, Tsvetan told Slavko that he had decided to join the Catholic Church with a view to becoming a priest. Whereas he did seek his opinion about becoming a priest he did not mention the issue of celibacy and certainly made no reference to Tatyana.

Slavko therefore limited his answer to the question he had been asked. "My dear young friend, if that is what you have decided for your life who am I to counsel against it. I know you as a thoughtful young man and you would have gone over your decision again and again, I am sure. I will give you only one piece of advice. It is possible to set off on this course without actually committing to it fully at this stage. You are a very young man and as you get a little older a lot could change for you. Go ahead and join the Roman Catholic Church. It is a noble enough institution. Go and study. All I ask is that you delay the final decision to become a priest for a few more years."

Tsvetan listened carefully, as always treating his mentor's advice with respect. "I understand what you are saying to me, but surely it makes no difference. I will join the Catholic Church; I will attend a suitable university and then I will become a priest."

"Exactly!" Slavko exclaimed. "So if it makes no difference you do not have to tie yourself to the decision at this stage. Also, you are forgetting a major factor. As far as I am aware you have not yet discussed this with your parents." Tsvetan acknowledged that this was indeed the case. "It will be enough of a shock to them that you want to leave the Orthodox Church and also that you are not willing to study at your home university. Why make it harder for them by also committing yourself to the priesthood?"

"But if I do not yet finally tie myself to the idea of the priesthood I will still carry that intention in my heart." said Tsvetan.

"Then carry it in your heart. The idea and the intent will be safe there." the old teacher replied. "You have made enough decisions about your future path for a young man yet to reach the age of maturity. I implore you to leave it there." Tsvetan nodded his assent. "Now go and give some thought to how you will approach your parents on this. It will not be easy."

It was not their custom to show physical warmth to each other, probably because they were first and foremost teacher and pupil. However, Tsvetan took a step towards the old teacher with an open gesture and Slavko spread his arms to receive the young man's hug. After a few moments the two men awkwardly released each other from their clumsy embrace.

"I envy you," said Slavko, still with his hands resting on Tsvetan's shoulders. "I am in the autumn of my life and certainly all ambition, although only partially fulfilled, is firmly in the past for me. I will gain much pleasure from watching your progress towards achieving your ambitions and I will be hoping for God's blessings upon you."

Reverting to normal behaviour they shook hands, said goodnight and parted to go their separate ways. As Slavko, walked home he thought about his own final words to Tsvetan. It was not entirely true that he had no more ambitions in life. He still longed for something for himself: the safe and happy return of Vesela, his beloved wife.

Chapter Four

Since his discussion with his teacher, Tsvetan had given further thought to his plans. Again he returned to the question of how his parents would manage to finance his study given his intention to seek a university place in a large city. This had taken him back to the idea of seeking a scholarship from the Catholic Church to study in Italy. Although his parents would be shocked at the idea of him leaving Bulgaria it would at least give him some independent means were his application for a scholarship to be successful. He could then supplement this income by working in the evenings or weekends.

Tsvetan had become aware that to get such a scholarship you were not required to commit yourself unequivocally to becoming a priest, although the granting of a scholarship was almost certainly dependent on the student having a strong interest in this particular path. At first he worried that this course of action would fly in the face of the promises that he had virtually given to his teacher. However, he finally concluded that it was consistent with what they had discussed. If his application for a scholarship was successful he would go to an Italian university to study theology and when his course of study was complete he would be able to make a well informed choice regarding the priesthood.

With his plans firmly made he decided to speak to his parents at dinner that night.

"What! Have you taken leave of your senses? Svishtov's most famous citizen, Dimitar Apostolov Tsenov, leaves his fortune to the town to build a wonderful university and you decide you want to study in Italy! It is an outrage. I won't hear of it." Tsvetan's father had gone bright red in the face. He could not even bring himself to look at his son, such was his disappointment in Tsvetan.

His mother looked at her husband with concern. "Calm down, Todor. You will have a heart attack at this rate. Firstly our son is no fool and secondly he has never brought worry to our door. Hear him out."

"I have heard enough of this madness," he replied, but thankfully made no move to leave the room.

Tsvetan's younger brother Grozdan looked on in amazement. His elder brother had some wild notions, but this one surpassed all others. Grozdan hated conflict, but could see that this argument was not heading for an easy conclusion.

Tsvetan listened, nervous and bewildered. He was frightened to say anything for fear he could make matters worse. For now he would leave his mother to advocate for him. How he regretted not talking to her first. By blurting it all out to the two of them together he had surprised her and weakened her ability to support him.

His father was not finished yet. "How are we supposed to manage the land and the fishing without him here?" he enquired of his wife, apparently giving up on hearing any sense from Tsvetan.

"When the boys were small we managed and we will manage again in the same way. Grozdan is already doing a lot of the jobs around the farm and by the time Tsvetan leaves for university he will be able to do more."

His wife's simple yet logical approach disarmed him and his younger son affirmed what she was saying. "Don't worry, Papa. I am happy to do more," he assured him.

Todor took another tack. "We are a Christian family brought up within the Orthodox Church, like our parents and grandparents before us. What about this nonsense of becoming a catholic? The next thing we know he will be saying he wants to be a catholic priest!" Wisely, Tsvetan held his tongue. "I forbid it. I forbid it all," his father continued. "I am going to get Father Yosif to speak to him. That is my final word."

"But, father he will not give me a fair hearing on converting to Catholicism. He will be even angrier than you." Tsvetan could see his whole enterprise folding before his eyes. He looked imploringly at his mother, but she said nothing. This was not the time to cross her husband.

His father glared at him. "You will speak to Father Yosif. Your mother and I will arrange it. Now go to your room."

Further argument would have been ill-advised. Getting up from the dinner table where the family still sat Tsvetan slunk away to the bedroom he shared with Grozdan. Wanting himself to get away and assuming his parents wanted to discuss the matter in private, Grozdan followed on behind his brother shortly afterwards.

When Grozdan arrived at their bedroom his brother was sitting on an old wooden chair staring out of the window. Grozdan spoke to his brother's back. "I have never seen father so vexed before," he said. "Why do you always have such crazy ideas? Even a saint would lose patience with you."

Tsvetan turned halfway towards his brother, but still kept at least one eye on the view beyond the window as if he was expecting salvation to walk up and knock on their door. His reply to his brother was intended to silence him.

"If you have nothing useful to say then keep quiet," he advised, but Grozdan was not going to be silenced so easily.

"It just so happens that I do have something very useful to say," he began. "For everyone's sake please just forget the whole thing. If you must go to university then attend the one here like any sensible person would," he added.

"Go to bed, Grozdan!" Tsvetan told him and there the conversation ended. Grumpily, Grozdan got undressed down to his underclothes and climbed into bed. He turned his back to his brother and for the first time that he could ever remember settled into his bed without saying goodnight.

*

"Milen, are you fishing today?" Tsvetan was calling across the street to his friend.

Milen's low baritone voice boomed back. "This afternoon, yes. My mother has given me some errands which will take up most of the morning. I'll see you at the boat."

Two hundred metres along the bald street Georgi Georgiev, a very elderly neighbour smiled to himself. He felt reassured. He had been worrying that his hearing was going, but had heard Milen as if he had been standing next to him. He recalled with affection his days on the same boat with Milen's grandfather. He was glad to hear that the old tub was still afloat.

With an uncanny almost telepathic understanding the two friends arrived at the boat within a few minutes of each other although no time had been agreed. At once Milen could sense that his friend had something on his mind. He seemed distracted and was nervously chewing his lower lip.

"What is it, Tsvetan? Something is troubling you I can tell. Has the lovely Tatyana turned her nose up at you after all?"

Tsvetan who had been the first to arrive continued to prepare the nets for the fishing trip. He spoke without looking up. "Many things are troubling me, so much so I hardly know where to start."

"Try starting at the beginning," Milen suggested. "It usually helps." Tsvetan allowed himself a brief smile. How lucky he was to have Milen as a friend. Milen had always maintained that his friend thought too much about everything and he was probably right. For Milen everything was so refreshingly simple.

The young men climbed into the boat and pushed off from the shore. They continued in silence until they were in the middle of the river and the nets were carefully laid out behind the vessel. Milen could sense that his friend was about to speak. He waited patiently.

"There are so many things bothering me, but yes you are right, first and foremost it is about Tatyana that I am fretting."

"You said you were going to talk to her," Milen interjected. "Have you not done so?"

"I went to see her, but I said nothing. The family are moving away. It is all too late." Tsvetan's voice trailed off as he looked down at the bottom of the boat.

Milen's quick riposte shook him from his self-pity. "What are you telling me? You went to see her and you said nothing? My mother told me this morning that the family are rumoured to be leaving for Plovdiv. So what! All the more reason to talk to her now. Tell her she can't go because it will break your heart. It is what she wants to hear, believe me."

"If only it were that easy," said Tsvetan resignedly. "They are leaving. I can't stop them."

"It is that easy. Don't be a bloody fool, or you will always regret it. For God's sake, man, do something!"

Tsvetan continued to look at the floor of the boat. His voice was little more than a mumble. "I am doing something," he replied. "I am going to become a priest."

"What! You are in love with a beautiful girl and rather than speak to her you are going to take an oath of celibacy? Give me a break, you stupid bloody idiot. I've had it with you."

"Well for someone who's washing their hands of me you've got a lot to say for yourself. You should learn to mind your own business. I've always had ambitions to be a priest. You know that."

"Yes, because you've always been a bloody idiot, that's why."

Tsvetan's last words had been deeply hurtful to Milen. His so-called friend had involved him in his troubles, as he so often did, and when he had told him what he thought he was informed it was none of his business. Milen's thoughts roamed from grabbing Tsvetan by the throat and dragging him to see Tatyana to just throwing him overboard and leaving him to drown. In the end he did nothing and said nothing.

Tsvetan was instantly aware that he should not have spoken to Milen in that way, but his friend's angry response had caught him off guard. Milen had never in their long friendship insulted him in that manner and it had shocked and angered him.

The two young men were aboard a small boat in close proximity to each other, but somehow they managed to undertake the necessary chores required without speaking or even meeting each other's eyes. Continually they brushed past each other or politely moved aside to let the other go by, but not a syllable passed their lips. They went more than an hour like this and then suddenly they both saw the absurdity of it. Simultaneously they each attempted a stumbling apology then both abruptly fell silent to allow the other one to speak. They stood staring at each other until at last Tsvetan embraced his friend.

"What a pair of idiots!" he exclaimed.

"Speak for yourself!" retorted Milen and they both smiled, at first hesitantly, then without holding back they laughed at their own folly.

Wanting something to distract themselves they hauled in the nets to examine their catch. The nets were empty.

"Well this is a great afternoon isn't it? We haven't even caught any bloody fish. So we can go home hungry as well as miserable," observed Milen.

"We could?" pondered Tsvetan "Or we could row over to Belene Island and put ashore for a few hours and just enjoy the birdsong."

Milen stroked his chin. "My friend that is an excellent idea."

Chapter Five

While the two friends headed for Belene Island Tsvetan's mother was at home deep in thought. She had been trying to avoid a conversation with her husband until she was clear what she thought about her son's bombshell and what she should say to them both. She had high ambitions for her son and certainly was not prepared to hold him back because of his duties at home. With the help of their younger son they would manage without him. She had long since suspected that Tsvetan had no interest in studying at the economic institute in Svishtov. It was not only that he had shown little interest in business and finance, but also that he always gave non-committal replies whenever the subject came up. Needless to say, her husband had picked none of this up.

Of course as a mother the idea that her eldest son might be moving to Italy was horrifying. She would potentially go years without seeing him. Surely there was some way through this, but while her husband was so wound up it would be difficult to make progress. In addition, her husband's decision to involve the local Orthodox priest in deciding the question of whether her son could convert to Catholicism was unlikely to end well. Father Yosif was a sweet man, but he was hardly likely to give Tsvetan a fair hearing on this particular subject. Besides, Tsvetan was one of the few young men in the town who could be regarded as a devout Christian and Father Yosif would not be keen to surrender him to another church. Before she spoke with her husband she needed to be completely clear on how her son had come to these decisions.

*

To get to Belene Island Milen and Tsvetan had needed to row against the river's current and by the time they put ashore they were good for nothing. However, they were fishermen to the bone and without even consulting on the matter they both set up fishing rods on the bank before doing anything else. Once the rods were in place they sat down on the banks and opened two bottles of beer that were always kept in the boat for just such an occasion.

"We should do this more often," said Tsvetan. "I had forgotten how beautiful the place is."

Milen's sense of humour had now been restored and his retort was typical of the man. "Yes we should, but next time remind me to bring an adequate rowing partner."

Tsvetan carried out a mock attack which Milen struggled to repel without spilling his beer which was his priority. "As I suspected," said Milen, "If you had been rowing properly you wouldn't have so much energy left."

The beautiful Belene Island is formed by the Danube River splitting into two branches passing north and south of it. The frontier between Bulgaria and Romania follows the north branch of the river and therefore Belene Island is part of the Bulgarian territory. Tsvetan and Milen had been sitting on the southern banks of the island facing the Bulgarian mainland, but they now found themselves strolling inland, exploring what the small and enchanting island had to offer. After just a few hundred metres the river had disappeared from view, lost behind a seemingly impenetrable screen of willow and poplar trees. Here the atmosphere was damp and heavy, and the friends could hear thousands of insects already active among the leaves. Occasionally the woodlands gave way to small patches of pasture interspersed with a wide variety of different coloured flowers. The sound of nearly two hundred different species of birds filled the air. Sometimes their songs created a melodic harmony and then, as if coordinated by an unseen conductor, they all fell silent only to slowly strike up again.

"Wherever you go, Tsvetan, and for however long you will surely miss this place," said Milen.

"I will miss this place and this moment and many moments of friendship just like it," his friend replied. "But I am going nowhere for a while. I don't want to think of leaving. I would certainly do so with a heavy heart just now with so much unresolved and my parents at my throat."

Milen stopped in his tracks and turned to look at Tsvetan. "Your parents at your throat? You must have given them cause. They are always on your side."

"I told them I wanted to study in Italy on a scholarship from the Catholic Church. Their reaction, or at least my father's, was similar to yours, just without the foul language."

Milen had by now assimilated his friend's plans and to him they seemed all over the place, but there was no point in starting another argument now. "I would gladly come to speak to your parents with you, you know that, but I think you need someone more sensible to sort this all out. Have you discussed any of this with old Nikolov?"

Tsvetan slowly walked on holding back a branch to stop it recoiling into his friend's face. "He knows of my plans, but I have not spoken to him since my fall out with my parents. Maybe I should?"

"You definitely should," Milen advised. "He will help in any way he can. We all know you are his favourite student."

Tsvetan did not argue this latter point because he knew it to be true. "I will. I will speak to him."

"Well I suggest you do it quickly," Milen added, "Before your old man blows a gasket."

When Tsvetan got home that evening the reception from his father was frosty, but no longer openly hostile. He very much regretted that he did not have a decent catch to please his father and lighten the atmosphere a little, but in that respect his day had been entirely unproductive. No doubt this simply reinforced his father's view that Tsvetan spent too much time dreaming. His father merely informed him, in a dispassionate manner that was very unfamiliar to Tsvetan, that Father Yosif would be calling in about an hour's time after the evening service. Tsvetan had no wish to speak with the priest and was somewhat taken aback that his father had gone ahead and arranged it all so quickly. However, he just acknowledged what his father had told him and otherwise said nothing.

*

Father Yosif stood in the hallway in his dusty vestments. Tsvetan noticed for the first time that his beard was now entirely grey contrasting with his jet black klobuk, the cylindrical hat that marked him out as an orthodox priest. Politely, but firmly he asked to speak to Tsvetan's father alone and, although both Tsvetan and his mother were unhappy about this, the priest and Tsvetan's father brushed off their objections and disappeared into the living room that was only used for receiving important guests like Father Yosif. Tsvetan and his mother sat at the kitchen table in silence. Grozdan, sensing more conflict, went to busy himself outside. Tsvetan waited anxiously while his mother sat fuming, at the same time not wanting to transmit her anger to her son.

Suddenly after about twenty minutes she rose purposefully from her chair, told Tsvetan to wait there and strode into the living room without knocking, which would have been customary in such a situation. To her dismay Father Yosif was just putting on his cape and making to leave.

"What is going on here, Todor? I thought Father Yosif was here to speak to Tsvetan, but he appears to be leaving."

Her husband looked unsure whereas Father Yosif made no move to stay. Buttoning his cape Father Yosif explained the outcome of the meeting to her as if she were the family's hired help.

"There is no need for me to see him. The matter is concluded. I have refused permission for him to leave the Orthodox Church and your husband and I have agreed he will finish his studies at the High School and then attend the Dimitar Apostolov Tsenov Academy for his degree. After that he would have reached the age of maturity and can make his own decisions. Goodnight to you both."

Tsvetan's father could see the lightning flash above his wife's head and now he was waiting helplessly for the thunderclap. His wait was not a long one.

"Thank you, Father for your advice, but I wish you to know that is all it is: advice. No one, and I mean 'no one' refuses permission to our son besides my husband and me and for your information I can tell you now that he is not attending the Dimitar Apostolov Tsenov Academy. As for him joining the Catholic Church that is a matter between him, God and his own conscience. My hope is that he does not take this course, but if he does do this against the advice of all three of us then so be it. Now Father, if your cape is securely buttoned I will show you out."

With that she led the shell-shocked priest through the kitchen, where the open mouthed Tsvetan still sat obediently, into the hall to the front door. By the time she returned to the living room her husband had regained what he thought was his authority.

As his wife entered the room he took up a pompous stance in front of the unlit stove and began to speak. "You have brought shame on this family. How could you speak to our local priest in that manner? I could hardly believe my ears."

"He's lucky I did not throw him out of the house," she retorted. "You are to blame for involving him in the first place."

This time her husband's blood pressure really was at risk. He opened his mouth to speak, but found himself addressing his wife's retreating form. She left the room, slamming the door as she went. A normally peaceful and harmonious family was in uproar and in danger of being permanently bruised.

Tsvetan was glad that the following day was a school day. He got up early and left for school before the family had properly stirred. He was saddened by the turn of events that had been set off following his revelations of how he saw his future. There was now an open wound between his mother and father and this upset him more than anything. It was his responsibility to put things right and he would start by taking Milen's advice.

He could not wait until the end of the day when he would have Slavko Nikolov's full attention. As his classmates went for lunch he went hungry and instead sought out the old teacher. However, when Tsvetan found him Slavko Nikolov was not inclined to give up *his* lunch quite so easily. On top of that his view was that it would do the boy no harm to hold on to his perceived problems for a few more hours. He was sometimes too intense for his own good. Anyway the lunch on Mondays was usually spinach balls in tomato sauce and he was not missing that for anyone.

"Go and have your lunch and I will see you tonight," he advised. "After all your parents have paid for it. We don't want you forgetting how well they look after you."

This last remark struck home as the wily old schoolmaster had intended. Tsvetan went back to join his classmates in the ancient dining room with its perpetual smell of cabbage. He felt chastened and would just have to hold himself together.

The older pupils ate at a huge round table slightly apart from the younger children and as Tsvetan approached they all instinctively shuffled round to make room for him next to Milen.

"Where have you been?" his friend enquired. "I've had to defend your spinach balls with my life.

"I'm not hungry," Tsvetan replied. "I've too much on my mind."

"In which case I'm glad I defended them," said Milen and before Tsvetan could change his mind he piled the spinach balls and the now slightly congealed tomato sauce onto his own plate. "Waste not want not," he chuckled and set about the unexpected bonus with renewed vigour.

"Does nothing in life worry you?" Tsvetan asked.

"Well, yes of course. I wish the tomato sauce wasn't quite so lumpy, but beggars can't be choosers," he quipped.

Tsvetan smiled to himself. How he envied Milen's perennial cheerfulness. How easy it must be not to feel the weight of the world bearing down on you. He must take a leaf out of Milen's book and try and lighten up if he was not going to worry himself into an early grave. In particular, it was not going to help him resolve things with his parent's if he remained wound up like a spring about to uncoil. Again he saw the wisdom of his teacher and mentor. It would do him good to think things through for himself as far as he could before hearing whatever advice Slavko Nikolov was about to give him. He would just have to wait until the end of school.

How familiar and reassuring this scene had become for Tsvetan. As he entered the teachers' staff room Slavko Nikolov looked up from his books and smiled at him. His hair was grey and dishevelled and his moustache was slightly discoloured from the gallons of strong black coffee he drank each day. His skin had become thinner with age, but his eyes still sparkled like two beacons of hope.

There were two other teachers still in the room although both had their jackets on and were about to leave. The room itself had not changed very much for many years. In the centre of the room a large pine table was scratched and stained from the effects of sharp writing implements and spilled drinks. None of the half a dozen or so chairs pulled up against the table matched, although the one occupied by Slavko Nikolov was of a superior design and comfort to the others denoting his age and status within the group. The whole room was imbued with what could best be described as a shabby cosiness, impregnated with the smell of coffee, tobacco and old suits. Both the remaining teachers liked Tsvetan and approved of how their colleague had taken him under his wing. They wished both Tsvetan and Slavko Nikolov a good evening and left together.

Slavko Nikolov directed his eyes to one of the chairs indicating that Tsvetan should sit down. He accepted the unspoken invitation and seated himself with as little fuss as he could muster given the weighty matters on his mind. Tsvetan was determined not to speak until invited to do so. Slavko was also doing everything he could to slow the young man down. Whatever he wanted from him it was obviously urgent in the young man's mind at least, but there was nothing to be gained from rushing at things like a bull in a china shop.

"Are you not reading my newspaper today?" Slavko asked him. "There is some very interesting, but rather shocking news about events in Italy."

"I know I should, sir," Tsvetan replied, "But there is so much on my mind I don't think there is room in my brain or my heart for more information. Not at least until I sort out the worries that are currently occupying me. I do really need your advice."

Slavko smiled to himself. Tsvetan was, despite his apparent maturity, just a boy. It is only when you are older that you develop the capacity to manage a whole plethora of anxieties at the same time.

"Have you spoken to your parents yet?" Slavko asked although it was abundantly clear that he had and it was the aftermath of this that he wanted to discuss.

Tsvetan confirmed that he had indeed spoken to his parents. He then proceeded to tell the whole story almost verbatim. He concluded by saying that he had been surprised and upset by the vehemence of his father's objections. He had also been at first disappointed that his mother had not taken his part in the original discussion with his father, although from what he had overheard from the kitchen it seemed that his mother had defended him stoutly against Father Yosif.

"Father Yosif walked past me in the kitchen with a face like thunder," Tsvetan confided with a mixture of pride and uncertainty.

Slavko Nikolov sat silent for a moment digesting everything his young student had said. When he eventually spoke Tsvetan was all the more attentive for having waited for what he had to say. A good teacher knows how to command attention and Slavko was certainly a very good teacher.

"If I had asked you three weeks ago whether you felt that your parents loved and supported you, what would you have said?"

Tsvetan looked at Slavko in a quizzical manner not sure where this conversation was going. "Of course I would have answered yes without hesitation," he said. "I love my parents and I know they love me."

Slavko stood up from the chair and started pacing around the room. Tsvetan's eyes remained focused on him. "And what if at the same time I had asked you for an opinion on Father Yosif, how would you have answered that query?"

Tsvetan was keen not to show a lack of respect to the local priest. "I would have said that he was a holy, God fearing man."

Slavko was not yet satisfied that his question had been fully addressed. "Would you have said he is a good man?"

Tsvetan's reply was immediate and emphatic. "Without question," he said.

"Then I have some good news for you," the shrewd old teacher announced. "Nothing has changed. Your parents think only of what is best for you and the good priest, Father Yosif, is guided by what he thinks God would want for you. You are lucky to have such excellent advocates, are you not?"

Tsvetan was confused. He had assumed all along that his teacher would take his side in this matter, but now he was not sure.

He could not think what to say. If he did not know Slavko Nikolov better he would be led to think that he had turned the argument against him. Slavko could sense Tsvetan's doubt. It was not hard; it was writ large on his young face.

"Let me ask you one final question," Slavko continued. "Do you also regard me as someone who will advocate on your behalf?"

Only ten minutes ago Tsvetan would have given an unequivocally positive response, now suddenly he was not sure. He was completely unable to read his teacher's intention. However, given everything that had happened between them over the last six months, there could only be one answer.

"Of course I do. I hope it does not sound impertinent, but I dare to think of you as my friend as well as my teacher."

"I am glad of it," Slavko replied. He knew he was giving the boy difficult choices, but if he was to speak on his behalf with his parents, then Tsvetan needed to trust him. Slavko knew that he would have some influence on the boy's parents, but was equally aware that he could not guarantee the outcome. "You are sure then that you trust me?" he asked.

"Of course I am sure," Tsvetan assured him.

"Then it is time to take up your mother's kind invitation to dinner."

Chapter Six

The dinner invitation was set for the following Friday and in the intervening days there was a tacit, but unspoken agreement between Tsvetan and his parents that they would not discuss any of this until then. Over the course of those days Tsvetan began to realise from their behaviour that his parents also wanted a resolution to this argument. Disagreement within the household was as unfamiliar and unpleasant to them as it was to him and each of them hoped that the teacher could help them find a way forward. For himself, Tsvetan had already decided that whatever came out of the discussion he would accept it. He had thought a great deal about the questions that Slavko Nikolov had put to him and had begun to understand what was behind them. Slavko Nikolov was simply helping him realise that people that love you can be on your side without necessarily agreeing with you. Tsvetan was therefore confident that a meeting between him and these three people, all of whom he loved dearly, could not really have a bad outcome.

*

"Well!" exclaimed Slavko Nikolov, addressing the whole family, "I have to say that was a wonderful meal and I have had the pleasure of your excellent company in sharing it with you. Thank you all so much."

"You are most welcome," Todor replied.

"Now I am aware that all of you were expecting me to say something about young Tsvetan's future as this has been the source of some unwanted and I gather unusual discord between you."

Tsvetan's mother was the first to answer, but only to defer to her husband. "I am glad you enjoyed the dinner. It has been lovely to have you here. Tsvetan talks about you constantly. You are welcome to come any time and we all hope you will find time for us again. But, yes we do have some things to sort out. We would appreciate your help, but I will leave it to my husband, Todor, to explain our worries to you."

Todor cleared his throat and then, having himself offered further hospitality to Slavko, gave a full account of their discussions and disagreements. Although he made it plain where he stood on the issues, he showed no sign of the anger he had expressed when first his son had spoken to them.

"I agree with my husband in every respect except one," Tsvetan's mother added when it was clear that her husband had finished speaking. "Todor and I have discussed this between us. The thing is I see no purpose in him attending an Academy dealing with business and economics. Tsvetan has never shown any interest in this and it seems he would rather not go to university at all than attend here in Svishtov. As Todor has said, a big problem for us is how to support him financially if he leaves home."

Slavko Nikolov was on the verge of replying when he noticed that Tsvetan was eager to speak. He sat back in his chair to indicate that he would defer to the young man.

"Mama that is why I suggested studying in Italy. The Catholic Church offers scholarships to good students. I feel confident that I would get one," he said looking to Slavko for affirmation that was not forthcoming.

Tsvetan's mother looked at her son with a gentleness that was hard to resist. "I know that, but if you go to Italy that would be hard for me as your mother to endure. It is so far from home."

Tsvetan's father then interjected in a more authoritarian tone than he had displayed hitherto. "Tsvetan, they will only take you if you convert to Catholicism and I forbid it at your age. What you do when you are older is up to you."

Slavko Nikolov decided that the time had come for a contribution from him. "I said to Tsvetan earlier this week that he should read what is happening in Italy. Italy's government has just passed some shocking laws which forbid Jews from Italian citizenship. It is an unstable country with the same attitudes that abound in Germany. You tell me all the time Tsvetan how you hate fascists. Well, Italy is run by fascists. You cannot go there, I think."

Tsvetan could not disagree, but was alarmed to see his options closing. His father Todor had little knowledge of the world and never read newspapers. He was finding it hard to follow and hoped that Slavko Nikolov would just offer a solution for them.

Slavko did indeed have a plan and now was the time to unveil it. "I think we have established that Tsvetan should not attend our academy here in Svishtov."

Todor was not sure that this was so, but said nothing.

Slavko Nikolov continued. "There are so many reasons that we have talked about to exclude Italy and this option should not trouble us further. As his schoolmaster, my view is simple. Tsvetan would make an excellent teacher and whatever he wants to do in life qualifying as a teacher will be a great asset how ever he chooses to serve God and the community. He should study to be a teacher at one of our best universities, Sofia, Tarnovo or Plovdiv. By far the best of these is Plovdiv. I recommend this course of action."

At the mention of Plovdiv Tsvetan pricked up his ears. He tried to catch his teacher's eye, but Slavko was not looking his way. Tsvetan was amazed at Slavko Nikolov's suggestion. Could he know about Tatyana? He was certain that he had never spoken to his teacher about it, but surely it was too much of a coincidence. Just as Tsvetan was starting to dream about a life in Plovdiv with Tatyana close by his father interrupted his reverie.

"I could agree to your idea, sir, but there remains the question of cost. I do not know how we would afford his lodgings in Plovdiv. I imagine it to be an expensive city."

Now that Plovdiv had been mentioned Tsvetan was not going to give up the idea without a fight. "You know father that I can live very modestly and I could work too." he implored. "I will manage somehow."

His father's heart was starting to melt. He loved his son and wanted him to be happy, but he knew that the boy was being unrealistic. "We are not prepared to send you to Plovdiv to starve," his father said emphatically. "Give me a moment to think."

That morning Todor had met Tatyana's uncle in town and Kalin had told him that his brother's family were giving up everything and moving to Plovdiv. Kalin had been very worked up about it and Todor felt for him, facing the loss of his only brother. He had not thought about it again until now. If anything could turn his son away from thoughts of being a catholic priest surely that girl could? She could turn any young man's head. Suddenly the idea of his son studying in Plovdiv had its advantages, but how to afford it?

Slavko Nikolov seemed to be reading his mind. "You are right to say that Tsvetan could not manage without some financial support, but I might be able to help." All eyes turned to Slavko Nikolov. Tsvetan wondered what else this miracle worker had up his sleeve. "The school holds a small bursary to use for very gifted students. It was left by a former pupil of the school in his will, but our Headmaster has never seen fit to use it up until now. I am sure that I could persuade him to use it to support Tsvetan. The Head has always been very impressed with him."

"But is it right that it should go to support our son, especially when there is a perfectly good academy here in the town?" Todor asked. "Surely it is for us to support him?"

Tsvetan looked crestfallen, but knew his father was only saying what any proud parent would think proper.

"It is my suggestion, on behalf of the school, that Tsvetan should study in Plovdiv and it is therefore appropriate that the school should offer some help to this end. Anyway, we have some leverage with the Headmaster," he added with a twinkle. "The Headmaster himself took his teaching exams at Plovdiv and thinks it is the only place worth attending."

Tsvetan stared at Slavko Nikolov in total admiration. He felt shame when he remembered the slight doubt he had felt when his teacher had asked whether he regarded him as someone who would advocate for him. A person could not have a more able and compassionate ally. His gratitude to his old mentor was incalculable.

Everyone thanked Slavko profusely as he rose to leave. Not forgetting his manners he again thanked Tsvetan's mother for the wonderful dinner, but the hosts assured him that it was they that needed to thank him. As he walked home Slavko felt a warm satisfaction. He had no doubt that his friend and colleague, the school's Headmaster would agree to his plan. However, Slavko had probably given the impression that the bursary would cover everything and he knew that was most likely not the case. Still, he had some small savings himself that he would happily use. Tsvetan and his family need never know.

Tsvetan was jubilant and despite it now being nearly ten in the evening he desperately wanted to go and tell his friend Milen. His mother was a little worried that the family might regard it as rather late to be calling, but his father told her she was just being silly.

"Leave the boy be," he told his wife. "It is like a second home to him. No one will mind."

Tsvetan was off like a flash and five minutes later he and Milen were sitting in Milen's yard like two conspirators.

"I can't believe he chose Plovdiv. If only he knew," said Tsvetan after relating the whole story.

Milen looked at him as if he could not believe what a naïve idiot his friend was. "Of course he knew. Everyone sees how you feel about Tatyana except her and everyone knows that she worships you. The old man is not blind."

Tsvetan looked at his friend in genuine amazement. "That can't be so," he said quietly.

"Of course it is so, you moron," replied Milen. "I think the old guy knows you pretty well, doesn't he?"

"Well, yes I guess he does."

"Well then," said Milen conclusively. "So what are you doing here? Go and tell her!" Milen directed.

Tsvetan put his head into the doorway of the old kitchen where he knew an ancient clock hung over the stove. "It is already half past ten," he reported. "She will probably be in bed."

"I can't think of a better place for her to be," replied his friend with a lewd smile across his face.

Tsvetan ignored him. "I will go to see her tomorrow, first thing," he said. He gave Milen a mock punch and left walking on air.

*

Tsvetan left the house at eight the next morning, unable to last another minute without sharing his news with Tatyana. As he approached her house he was a little surprised to find the place so quiet. He feared the family had not yet risen, although this would be very unusual in Svishtov where most families virtually rose with the sun. Then he heard someone sweeping in the yard and his anxiety disappeared. He headed for the yard where to his surprise he found Tatyana's uncle. Kalin looked up from his broom and greeted Tsvetan less than warmly.

"What are you looking for here, Tsvetan?" he enquired with the air of a man who knew the answer to his own question.

"Is Tatyana at home?" asked Tsvetan politely.

"No one is at home. They left for Plovdiv early this morning." Tsvetan froze.

"That can't be!" he exclaimed desperately. "I need to speak to her. I have news."

The uncle looked at him without pity. "Well, you will have to keep your news to yourself," Kalin retorted. "That snob of a woman has taken them all to her beloved Plovdiv leaving me without a brother." Apparently unaware how much pain he had already inflicted on the boy Kalin added. "That poor girl! My dear niece Tatyana left here sobbing."

*

Although on the face of it Slavko Nikolov had little to get up for, he was in his kitchen before six that morning with a broad smile on his face. He had a cup of coffee in his hand and on the table before him stood, by his meagre standards a sumptuous breakfast. He put down his cup and filled his mouth with some of the bread and sausage that Tsvetan's mother had insisted he took home with him. He was now glad that he had accepted the generous gesture. She was obviously a fine baker as well as an excellent cook. The home-made bread was the best he had tasted in a very long time. Following the success of his enterprise on behalf of young Tsvetan Slavko felt invigorated. He was determined to make good use of this new buoyant and optimistic mood. He would re-commence the search for his missing wife.

Chapter Seven

Eighteen Months Later

Milen and Tsvetan had decided that they would spend their last day together fishing on Belene Island. On the following morning Tsvetan would be leaving very early to travel to Plovdiv whereas Milen would be staying in Svishtov and in just a week he would be starting as an undergraduate at the Dimitar Apostolov Tsenov Academy. Both boys had long since known that they would be parting company at this time, but it had not made it any easier. However, they had said all there was to say on the subject and there was no point being maudlin about it. After all they both had plenty to look forward to and as they settled on the shore to bait and cast their fishing rods the conversation turned to the future.

"Will you look for her when you get to Plovdiv?" Milen asked.

Tsvetan had been expecting this question for months, but was still uncertain how to answer. "I have thought about that for so long, but I am still not sure what I will do, if anything. Tatyana's uncle gave me the address that they moved to, but other than receiving a letter to say they arrived OK, he has heard nothing. That was more than a year ago."

"Don't you find that strange?" Milen asked looking at his friend for any signs to indicate how he felt, but detecting none.

"Not really," Tsvetan replied. "I mean it is the women that usually keep in touch and from what I can gather Tatyana's mother and aunt did not part the best of friends."

Milen was quiet for a moment. He had promised himself he would not start going on about Tatyana, but when it came to it he could not hold back. "You missed your chance with her once before. Don't do it again," he implored.

"I am sure she has no further interest in me," replied Tsvetan. "She will probably have a host of rich suitors or even a husband. Anyway, I am going there to study."

Just at that moment there was a sharp tug on Tsvetan's line and both boys turned their attention to the fishing. Tsvetan was grateful for the distraction. His rod was now forming an arc and he was not finding it easy to land the fish.

"Christ, you must have a crocodile on the end of that!" Milen exclaimed. "Let it run. It will wear itself out."

Tsvetan did as his friend suggested, but was alarmed to see his reel whizzing around as if powered by electricity. Suddenly the fish appeared above the water, dived again and tore away, breaking the line as it went.

"My God, did you see it? It was a sturgeon. It was over a metre long!" Milen yelled out in a state of frenzied excitement. "I haven't caught a sturgeon in years."

"I've never caught one and now maybe I never will. I made a right hash of that," said Tsvetan, obviously disappointed with himself.

"Don't be daft," said his friend. "These rods are designed for catching carp or trout, not monsters like that. Forget it, Tsvetan. Let's have a beer."

Both friends enjoyed a beer, but neither of them were drinkers. On this occasion, however, they drank more than was sensible given the need to get back to the mainland. Eventually they did set off from the island, but were only about halfway home when the wind started up suggesting a storm was imminent. This soon sobered them up and they rowed for all they were worth arriving at the shore just as the heavens opened.

"I am going to worry about you when I am gone," said Tsvetan. "With Nicholai or Dido you would never have got home."

Milen smiled. "I would have managed OK with Dido," he maintained. "If I had been with Nicholai I would have just thrown him overboard and rowed home alone."

Both friends laughed. Despite the rain the day had turned out as each of them had hoped.

*

"Is the boy ready?" the baker enquired with a clear expectation that he would not be. It was three thirty in the morning and Tsvetan was travelling with him on his early morning run to Veliko Tarnovo.

"He has been ready for over an hour," his mother reported. "It is me who is not ready. I don't want him to go, Stoyan, but what can I do?"

"You can do nothing. The boy must venture out in the world. It is the way of things these days," replied the baker.

"I know, but if he was just going to Tarnovo it would not be so bad. Plovdiv is so far."

The baker was sympathetic, but also realistic. "Gone is gone. It makes no difference how far it is. You wouldn't see him until next summer either way."

Tsvetan's mother looked mortified and was on the edge of tears when he appeared with his bags. His father, Todor, was only two paces behind him.

"Now don't take on so, my dear," Todor said to his wife. "We should feel very proud today. I certainly do."

"And so do I," his mother snivelled and then burst into floods of tears. Tsvetan said nothing, knowing that no words could help. Instead he gave his mother a tight hug, shook his father's hand and climbed into the old van alongside Stoyan.

"I will write," he promised and the baker, sensing there was little point in delaying the inevitable, put the van into gear and drove off with no more than a cursory wave.

Tsvetan dozed most of the way to Veliko Tarnovo which suited the baker as he was used to travelling in silence and liked it that way. As they drew close to the historic and beautiful town Tsvetan started to stir.

"Well you turned out to be good company," the baker joked. "Anyway, we will be there soon. Do you know where you are to catch the bus from?"

"I was told it was near the castle at Tsarevets, but I do not know where that is," Tsvetan replied. "I think the only time I have been there was with my parents when I was about eight," he added by way of an apology.

"I will do my best to find it," said Stoyan, although he knew exactly where the bus stop was. Teasing the boy helped to pass the time. Minutes later he pulled up alongside the bus, leaned across his young passenger and opened the door. "Good luck, Tsvetan. Don't talk to any strangers, especially pretty women," he advised and laughed out loud as he turned the van around and drove away.

The bus stop was in a large square where two roads descending from the centre of town came to an end. On the other side of the square a raised path alongside the River Yantra led to the arched entrance to Tsarevets castle. Tsvetan could see the ancient fortress looming above him, dominating the skyline.

He was not sure what he had expected, but the waiting bus looked ancient. He was at once glad that he was only travelling on it as far as Stara Zagora. He hoped that it would at least hold together for that distance. Although the bus was not due to leave for another twenty minutes he climbed aboard and settled into his seat. He was now for the first time starting to feel hungry.

It was still very early and eating his lunch seemed a bit foolhardy, but he had eaten breakfast at three that morning so it was not altogether unreasonable. When he opened the bag of food that his mother had made for him he realised he need not have worried. A whole army could have survived the day on what she had packed for just one person's lunch. Tsvetan tried to form a smile, but it did not materialise. For the first time, and quite suddenly, he realised just how much he was going to miss her. Instead a small tear formed in his eye. His mother was right. Plovdiv was a long way from home.

*

Slavko was lying in bed wondering how far his young friend had got on his long journey to Plovdiv. These days he was increasingly reluctant to get up and it was habit rather than any enthusiasm for the day ahead that caused him to rise. For the boy's sake he was genuinely pleased that everything had fallen into place and that Tsvetan was starting a new and exciting life at Plovdiv University, but for him it simply served to increase his loneliness. How he would miss Tsvetan coming into the staff room at the end of the school day.

Originally the reason had been to read his teacher's newspaper, but it soon developed into just an opportunity for discussion with the older man doing his best to guide his earnest young pupil's thinking on a range of issues. He could and did take some pride in the fact that Tsvetan now held fast to an open and liberal set of values that set him apart from others of his generation. His openness would be a great asset in his studies at Plovdiv and Slavko felt sure it would not be too long before his tutors at the university identified him as one to watch.

For the past year Slavko had been actively looking into the strange disappearance of his wife and at first his endeavours had seemed as if they might bear fruit. However, recently the trail had again gone cold and he was forced to admit that he was no closer to finding Vesela than he had been twelve months ago. Shortly after he resumed his search Vesela's sister had revealed a letter that she had received just days before his wife's disappearance. Although she did not say goodbye in the letter it had a tone of finality, for example setting right small disagreements the sisters had harboured. This told him that her disappearance was planned or at least expected. He gave this information to the police, but if anything it made them less interested in what had happened to her. The existence of the letter did at least give him cause to believe that she was still alive. At this moment that was all he had to sustain him.

*

Milen was also thinking about Tsvetan. Certainly he would see his oldest friend less, but he had been anticipating Tsvetan's departure for some time and would adjust to his absence just fine. When Tsvetan came home for the summer vacation they would no doubt take up with each other as before. He was confident that this would be the case for several years to come. What bothered him was the feeling that they stood at some sort of crossroads. He feared it was inevitable that eventually they would take different directions, so different that it would destroy their friendship. Try as he might he could not get this feeling out of his head. For now though he had a new start to look forward to. In a few days' time he would be attending one of Bulgaria's newest academies and he intended to grasp this opportunity with both hands.

Chapter Eight

Tsvetan was at last close to the end of his journey. The last leg, by train from Stara Zagora to Plovdiv had been the most comfortable. The train had only stopped three times and he was arriving in Plovdiv with plenty of time to have a good look around. The train came to a halt and all the passengers alighted this being the final stop. As he stepped onto the platform the size and the bustle of the station told him that this was a city on a scale that he had never encountered before. According to his teacher, Slavko Nikolov, Plovdiv had a population of more than one hundred thousand, compared to Veliko Tarnovo, with which he was a little more familiar, which had only fifteen thousand residents. It was a beautiful day without a cloud in the sky. The September sun was warmer than he had expected and Tsvetan stopped for a minute to take off a layer of clothing. With great anticipation he headed for the station exit from which the vast city opened out before him.

The most overwhelming impression was of the sheer number of people going about their business. Overfull buses chugged past giving off plumes of smoke from their blackened exhaust pipes. Trams, also crammed with people clattered along the tracks that seemed to criss-cross in every direction. Pedestrians walked across the tracks, apparently with little care for their own safety even as the trams bore down on them seemingly giving no quarter to those on the ground.

Tsvetan was also struck by the apparently contrasting fortunes of the citizens of Plovdiv. On the one hand he saw a number of fashionable ladies walk by wearing mid-calf length cotton dresses with shoulder pads and crossover necklines. Some of them carried an open parasol while others wore brimmed hats, often worn at an angle. They looked sleek and wealthy and completely unaffected by the shortages brought about by the approach of war.

They seemed not to notice those at the other end of the social scale openly begging on the same streets. Outside a stylish restaurant he saw a pretty young woman methodically going through the contents of a rubbish bin carefully retrieving anything that looked as if it might be edible. The well-heeled diners paid her no heed.

Taking all of this in Tsvetan walked slowly towards what the neat little signs indicated to be the old town. When he reached the older part of the city the crowds of people thinned out somewhat and he was able to take in the renaissance architecture that dominated this part of Plovdiv. Feeling at once at home he sought out a small café and sat down to enjoy a coffee and a cheese banitsa. Tsvetan had never experienced a city of such contrasts. He was going to find life in Plovdiv very interesting indeed.

After thirty minutes of just relaxing and taking in the atmosphere of Plovdiv Tsvetan decided he needed to find his digs and get himself settled. He rooted in his pockets for the address of the lodgings which would be his home for the foreseeable future.

He called the waitress across and paid his bill. "Do you by any chance know Bogomil Street?" he asked her. She was about his age and quite pretty. He tried to smile in a way that was friendly rather than flirtatious. From the coy way she looked at him it appeared that he was not entirely successful.

"Who wants to know?" she asked in response.

"I do," he replied feeling suddenly unsure of himself.

She laughed at his naivety. "Don't you have a name?" she continued although she was fast getting past caring.

Now feeling silly he answered her too earnestly. "Tsvetan, my name is Tsvetan."

"Well, Tsvetan," she began intentionally over articulating his name. "It is near the university. Do you know where that is?" He confessed he did not although he was about to become a student there. She looked him up and down, deciding she was wasting her time with a country hick. Finally she gave him directions to the university and from there to Bogomil Street. He thanked her a little too profusely and left the café in a cold sweat, hoping that all the girls in Plovdiv were not that hard to deal with.

Tsvetan followed the girl's directions which turned out to be pretty accurate and twenty minutes later he was standing outside the house where his parents had arranged accommodation for him. It was a tidy, unpretentious little house with a small front garden entirely given over to the growing of vegetables. A well-established grapevine climbed up the wall of the house supported by a heavy metal trellis.

Tsvetan looked again at his piece of paper. "Mrs Marinova, 37 Bogomil Street." This was it. He walked up the narrow path, just about visible between the spinach and the still flowering bean plants. He stood in front of the door examining it for a bell or knocker. Before he had discovered a means of announcing himself the door opened. A slim woman in her late forties appeared in the doorway. She stood erect with her shoulders back and her head held high on a slender neck. Her eyes looked straight into his not veering to left or right. He found this disarming and his well-rehearsed introduction faltered as a result.

"Good afternoon. Is it, am I speaking to Mrs...?"

Impatiently she finished his sentence for him. "Marinova and you will be Tsvetan. Is that all your luggage?"

By now he should have realised that a simple 'yes' would have sufficed, but instead he started to go into detail about what he had brought and what he had decided to leave at home. She continued to look at him and his voice trailed off into an indiscernible mumble.

"Well never mind that. Get yourself inside and let me have a look at you," she commanded. Tsvetan stepped forward wondering how her already deep scrutiny of him could possibly go up a gear. However, it seemed that this was just an expression she used because as soon as he set foot in the hallway she turned away from him and strode towards the staircase. "Follow me," she said. "I will show you your room."

An hour later Tsvetan sat alone in his room slightly overwhelmed by the intensity of his new landlady. She had very clearly laid out the rules by which he must live and, in particular, the restrictions that he needed to adhere to. The biggest emphasis was on the 'no visitor' rule from which Mrs Marinova said there was only one exception, which was a visit from his parents. "And no sisters!" she had added with emphasis. "How stupid do you think I am?"

Tsvetan did not think her at all stupid, just rather formidable. Missing her point entirely he had been at pains to let Mrs Marinova know that he did not have a sister.

The arrangement was that Tsvetan would have his breakfast and evening meals with Mrs Marinova and he was already regretting that his parents had not simply rented a room for him and left him to fend for himself. He was used to pleasant meal times at home with affectionate banter passing between him, his brother and his parents. He could only imagine that mealtimes here in Bogomil Street would be rather sombre affairs.

When it got to six in the evening and Mrs Marinova called him for dinner he feared the worst. She indicated where he should sit and much to his surprise placed on the table a freshly made Shopska salad and a small jug of rakia with two glasses. What was even more surprising, his landlady seemed to have undergone a complete personality change.

"I hope you will be very happy in Plovdiv," she announced with no lack of ceremony and raising her glass wished him good health. "Nazdrave!" Mrs Marinova exclaimed clinking her glass against his.

Tsvetan replied with enthusiasm. "Nazdrave!" And was the recipient of the broadest of smiles from his landlady who suddenly appeared quite attractive.

Tsvetan recalled a piece of advice given to him by Slavko Nikolov to be employed the first time he stood before a class. "Go in hard. Leave them in no doubt who is in charge. Once you have established your authority you can lighten up a bit later on." It seemed to him that Mrs Marinova adhered to the same philosophy, although he was amazed that the softer side of her should be revealed quite so soon. His good fortune continued as the salad was followed by a moussaka made in the Bulgarian way with potatoes, eggs and minced pork.

"We do not want you writing to your mother saying I don't feed you," she said with a twinkle in her eye. That, Tsvetan thought to himself, was extremely unlikely.

Chapter Nine

Tsvetan had now been in Plovdiv for nearly a month. With almost uncontrolled excitement he had registered in his first week and had now spent his first three weeks as a student at the university's education faculty. It met all his expectations and although at first a little overawed he had settled into university life almost seamlessly. Tsvetan was pleased to note that at least half the students were from outside Plovdiv and even a few of them were from his own Veliko Tarnovo Province. Inevitably his first friends came from this latter group.

At first a number of students who hailed from the city used their knowledge of the place to give themselves an added status within the group and some of them behaved in a rather condescending manner towards the newcomers. Others, however, tried to be as helpful as possible reducing the need for those from outside Plovdiv to continually seek advice from university staff for which both students and staff were grateful. In the end the group that had held themselves somewhat aloof from their fellows started to loosen up realising that they were in danger of isolating themselves from the other students. Once everybody settled down and stopped worrying about the impression they were making Tsvetan realised that he was a member of a very good natured and able group of scholars.

Tsvetan had spent the first few weekends sitting around in bars and cafes getting to know his new friends which he had very much enjoyed, but when another weekend arrived Tsvetan determined that the time had come to do a bit of sightseeing. In the first instance he decided to visit the second century Roman city for which Plovdiv was famous. Looking more like a tourist than a student he set off clutching a guide book loaned to him by Mrs Marinova and an old camera that his little brother had bequeathed to him as a going away present.

The old Roman city was magnificent and it was quite astounding how well preserved most of the structures were. Standing in the ancient stadium, once the venue for athletics as well as music and poetry contests, he was overwhelmed with the thought that so many people had stood here before him and wondered what sort of life each of them had led.

Life was so short it would be easy to let it pass by without significance or meaning, but in the short time allowed to him he was determined to make his life count, perhaps as a teacher, maybe as a priest. Those who had advised him thus far had been correct. It was enough at this stage to embark on a serious path without needing to plot the whole course.

Now reasonably established in the city it was inevitable that his thoughts would turn to Tatyana. He had received two letters from home, a long one from his mother and a very short missive from Milen. Both letters contained the same question: have you seen Tatyana? Having no experience of living in a city the size of Plovdiv his mother had expected that he would have bumped into her by now. The short note from Milen was aimed differently. Have you looked up Tatyana and if not, get on with it. He smiled as he thought about Milen. His advice was always simple and direct, but it had to be said: if Tsvetan had taken more notice of his friend's advice things could well be quite different now.

Tatyana and her family had moved into a house in Boulevard Maritza and having lived in Plovdiv a month Tsvetan knew that the boulevard ran along the opposite bank of the Maritza River that intersected the city. It was only a short walk from where he stood, crossing the bridge at Tsar Boris III Boulevard would take him straight onto it. He set off uncertain of the reception he would find there. He was aware that the information from Tatyana's uncle only gave the address to which they had originally moved and that the uncle had not heard of them since then. However, having endured the upheaval of moving from Svishtov it was unlikely that the family would have moved again. He therefore felt reasonably confident of finding them still in residence there.

Twenty minutes later Tsvetan had crossed the bridge and was walking along Boulevard Maritza looking for number 131. As he came closer the muscles in his stomach tightened and his nerve almost failed him, but having come this far he would pursue his mission to the end. Once he saw her, he told himself, he would know what to say. At this precise moment he had no idea beyond hello, how are you. He found number 127, but the next house along the road was number 141. At first he was confused, but then he noticed that set back from the road were half a dozen smart town houses on a small patch of green. He approached and these houses were indeed the missing numbers. Number 131 was less well kept than the neighbouring properties and soon to his great disappointment it became obvious that the house stood empty. The small front garden was overgrown and a wooden gate hung loosely on just one hinge.

With a heavy heart Tsvetan approached the house and peered through the windows. There were a few older items of furniture, a coal bucket lying on its side and some curtains on just one window. It was quite clear that no one had lived here for some time. Tsvetan felt desolate. It seemed that he was fated never to find Tatyana. Milen would no doubt think that again he was himself to blame for this and maybe he was. As he was about to walk away one of the neighbours came out of her house to peg up some washing. Tsvetan was not skilled at approaching strangers, but was desperate for some news about Tatyana and her family.

"Excuse me," he called. "Did you know the Kovachev family? I believe they lived here."

The woman looked across at him and then turned back to continue hanging up her washing. After a few seconds still with her back to him she replied.

"Who is asking?" she said.

"I am a friend of the family from Svishtov. I recently came to live here in Plovdiv and wanted to look them up."

The woman pegged out the garments that she already had in her hands and then turned to face him. She looked him up and down. He looked like a decent enough young man.

"As you can see you are too late. They have gone; to Sofia I believe. They left in a bit of a hurry." The woman could see the disappointment in the young man's face and her manner eased a little. "Yordana and her daughter Tatyana left about six months ago. I am sure they said they were going to Sofia. It is a shame. They were good neighbours."

Tsvetan could not understand. Something must have happened and what about Tatyana's father? "So is Mr Kovachev still here?" he enquired although he doubted that this could be the case.

The neighbour hesitated, not wanting to be the purveyor of bad news. However, he had to be told. She steeled herself and looked straight at Tsvetan. "Did you not know? He died about three or four months after they arrived here; from a heart attack. It was a terrible tragedy. He was no age to speak of."

Tsvetan lowered his head in anguish. For some time he said nothing. The woman continued to study him, feeling increasing sympathy for this young stranger, the first person to enquire after the Kovachev family since they had left. She guessed correctly which member of the family he was most interested in.

"Are you a friend of Tatyana?" she asked now with real compassion in her voice.

"Yes," Tsvetan replied. "She was so fond of her father. She must have been so upset," he added.

"She was," the neighbour confirmed. "They both were. It was particularly hard for Yordana. She blamed herself for bringing them here, but that was silly. These things just happen, often out of the blue." She could see that the young man was in a state of shock and the rest of her story was not going to make things any easier for him. "Come into the house." she suggested. "I can make you a cup of coffee."

Leaving her washing basket where it stood she led Tsvetan inside. They entered the kitchen where a well-used copper kettle stood on a blackened hob. She indicated a chair at the head of a huge wooden table and Tsvetan dutifully sat down. No words were spoken as the neighbour busied herself with the coffee. Eventually the coffee pot and two enamel mugs were placed on the table with a plate of sweet pastries. The woman poured the coffee and took up her story.

"After her husband died Yordana was like a ship without a rudder. She took it hard. The guilt began to eat away at her and she became quite strange. Her family, I am sure you know, live here in the town. They were very supportive at first, but as she became more reclusive they seemed to give up on her." She could see the tears welling up in the young man's face suggesting to her that he and Tatyana had been more than just friends.

"And what of Tatyana?" he asked. "How did she take it?"

"It is hard to say," she replied thoughtfully. "She had so much on her mind, what with the wedding coming up." She looked at him to gauge his reaction. As she expected, he looked totally crestfallen.

"So Tatyana is married now?" he asked with almost no hope in his voice.

"No, that is just it. That is why they left. She was engaged to be married to a rich industrialist twice her age, but she jilted him at the altar. I don't think she ever loved him. While he stood in the church she and her mother got a few of their personal items together and left."

Tsvetan had not touched his coffee nor had he even looked at the pastries. "Drink your coffee." The neighbour advised. "You look like you have seen a ghost."

Obediently, Tsvetan picked up his mug and drank some coffee. Feeling the strong black liquid doing him good, he then drained the mug and replaced it clumsily on the table.

"I know it is all so hard to take in," the woman said with genuine sympathy. Tsvetan merely nodded. For the time being he found nothing to say. "Just one last thing." the woman continued. "A letter came to the house no more than a fortnight ago. The postman did not know what to do with it so he asked me to take it. I opened it and it was from Yordana's brother in law enquiring after the family. He did not know that his brother was dead. It appears that Yordana had not told him."

Tsvetan's vacant gaze seemed to go right through the neighbour as if he was focusing on something behind her. "He did not know," he said at last. "It was he who gave me this address only a month ago."

The woman straightened in her chair. "He knows now," she said. "I felt it my Christian duty to write to the poor man and tell him what had happened. I told him that his brother had died and that Yordana and Tatyana had moved to Sofia."

"It was kind of you to do that and you have been more than kind to me as well," Tsvetan told her. "I am sorry to have taken up so much of your time." He took a scrap of paper and a pencil from the inside pocket of his jacket. He had brought the pencil and paper along in case he wanted to note anything down from his visit to the Roman city. He scribbled on the paper and handed it to the neighbour. "This is where I live in Plovdiv. I am a student here. If you hear anything from them I would be really grateful if you could let me know. My name is Tsvetan. I am not sure I introduced myself. I am sorry."

"It is not a problem, Tsvetan, and I am Bilyana, Bilyana Tomova. I will of course let you know if they get in touch, but I must say I do not expect it."

Tsvetan thanked her again, shook her hand and left, his world turned upside down.

Walking home he could hardly digest all that he had been told. He felt desperate for the family. From their time in Svishtov he knew them as a contented and harmonious family unit. Now through the death of the father they had been split asunder and languished in a large unknown city miles from their family. For him and Tatyana this was surely the end, if indeed there had ever truly been a beginning. The feelings Tsvetan encountered on hearing of their woes had made him realise the strength of his feeling for her, but now there was nothing to be done. He would never see her again.

Chapter Ten

Back in Svishtov Tatyana's Uncle Kalin was devastated to hear of the death of his brother, made worse by the fact that he had learned of it through a letter from a stranger almost a year after it had happened. His grief and anger were directed against Tatyana's mother whose determination to take the family away from Svishtov was, as far as Kalin was concerned, the cause of his brother's death. There was a lot of sympathy in Svishtov for Kalin and his family, but very little for Yordana. In her absence Yordana's reputation, in a town that had never quite taken to her, suffered badly.

All this came to the notice of Milen's parents and soon after Milen himself. He worried for his friend who surely had heard this terrible news and no doubt believed Tatyana to be lost to him forever. Milen and Tsvetan had shared all their highs and lows since they were small children and he was not about to allow his friend to suffer alone. Less than two weeks after Tsvetan's fateful visit to the abandoned house Milen was on his way to Plovdiv.

Unlike Tsvetan before him, Milen did not make a song and dance about arriving in the city. He got off the train, walked along the platform and, having shown his return ticket at the barrier, he stopped to consult his street plan. He had already marked both the train station and Bogomil Street on his map. He held the map open until he was outside the station and, having orientated himself, he set off for Tsvetan's lodgings at a brisk walk.

Milen had written to say he was coming, but with no real expectation that the letter would precede him and so it turned out. Unexpectedly at four o clock on a Saturday afternoon he appeared at the house in Bogomil Street. The door was opened by Mrs Marinova who eyed Milen suspiciously. In contrast to Tsvetan when he first encountered his landlady, Milen was not in the least bit unnerved by her.

"Good afternoon. My name is Milen. I have come to visit Tsvetan. Is he at home?" His posture was of a young man who demanded respect. Nevertheless, the landlady made no move to admit him, although she did at least confirm that Tsvetan was indeed at home. "It is good that he is here," Milen continued and then delivered his winning line. "I have a parcel from his mother."

Mrs Marinova stood aside. "You had best come in," she said.

As they both stood in the hallway Mrs Marinova turned to project her voice up the staircase. "Tsvetan!" she called. "You have a visitor."

Almost at once Tsvetan appeared at the top of the stairs. When he saw his friend standing there he was overjoyed. Then remembering Mrs Marinova's strict rule regarding visitors his joy turned to anxiety. He looked at her for guidance.

"You had best take your friend into the living room," she said with no hint of disapproval. "I will make you some coffee."

Tsvetan gave his friend such a hug he was almost overpowered. Mrs Marinova smiled to herself and turned towards the kitchen. Tsvetan led his friend into the living room as if he were entering a holy place.

"This is the first time I have ever been in here," he confided. "I don't think Mrs Marinova uses it either, not since I've been here anyway."

Milen looked around the room. Although the furniture was old it was of a good quality and had been well looked after. The room was spotlessly clean, although a little cold.

"You have landed on your feet here, my friend," Milen observed. "And your landlady seems alright. How have you been getting on?"

"Fine, just fine," Tsvetan replied. "The university is all I had hoped it would be and I have made a few friends, mainly from our province. How about you? How are your family?"

Milen smiled reassuringly. "We are all well. More to the point I have a letter from your mother... and a parcel. I called on your parents yesterday. They are very well and send their love."

On hearing about his parents Tsvetan relaxed visibly. He took the parcel that Milen held out to him. "I'd best not open it for the moment. It will be a food parcel and Mrs Marinova will be insulted."

Milen laughed at his friend's caution. Nothing changes, he thought. "She feeds you up does she? I thought you were getting a bit plump," he joked.

"I probably am," he confessed. "She puts enough on the table for five people, eats almost nothing herself and then sits and encourages me to finish everything."

Milen laughed out loud. "From the look of your stomach you seem to be doing as you're told," he replied. Instinctively Tsvetan looked down at his belly. Milen laughed even louder. "I had forgotten what an easy target you are," he said.

With Milen laughing happily and Tsvetan wearing a look of mock indignation, Mrs Marinova entered the living room with the coffee. Tsvetan observed with pleasure that she had three cups on the tray.

*

Milen's visit had been a real tonic to Tsvetan. They had spent a really enjoyable weekend looking around the city, meeting up with Tsvetan's new friends and sharing a few drinks in the evening. Mrs Marinova had made a mockery of her own rules and allowed Milen to sleep on an old mattress on the floor in Tsvetan's room. During their time together they spoke a great deal and, after exchanging news from home, their discussion had inevitably turned to Tatyana and what had befallen her family. Tsvetan told Milen about his visit to the house and his meeting with the kind neighbour. Milen told him about the sorrow felt by Tatyana's uncle and his family on hearing of the father's death, but was sparing with regard to how the town had turned against Tatyana's mother even in her absence.

Ironically Milen had come to try and persuade his friend not to give up on Tatyana, but his visit had the opposite effect. Tsvetan had told Milen that he was not going to pursue the matter any longer, pointing out that she had been close to marrying. Whatever her future is, he had declared to his friend, it is not with me. Milen tried telling him not to give up, citing the fact that she jilted her fiancé at the last minute as evidence that she could not forget Tsvetan. Tsvetan did not buy this and it soon became clear to Milen that he was wasting his breath. This time, unlike in the past, he was prepared to let it go. His friend had been suffering and he had come. That was enough. Anyway he could see clearly that his visit had helped Tsvetan so he left for Svishtov in the certain knowledge that the trip had been worthwhile. He would be able to tell Tsvetan's parents quite truthfully that their eldest son was doing fine.

From Tsvetan's point of view Milen's visit had helped put the past behind him. He was a new student at a highly respected university and he had much to look forward to. He recalled his discussion with his old teacher, Slavko Nikolov about not rushing into the decision to become a Catholic priest. It had been good advice. Although he believed he would in the end become a priest for the moment he was enjoying training to be a teacher.

Chapter Eleven

So rare was it for Slavko Nikolov to receive mail, the postman knocked on his door and delivered it to him personally. Slavko took the letter from him and thanked him politely. He sent his regards to the postman's father, an old friend, and gently closed the door. The postman, who was interested to know who the letter was from, walked back up the path his curiosity unsated.

It was a small envelope about the size of a postcard and from what Slavko could tell contained no more than a couple of thin sheets of paper. He turned it over in his hands examining the letter carefully. His name and address adorned the front of the envelope, but to his surprise the address was typed giving him no opportunity to identify the sender from the handwriting. Equally frustrating there was no address for the sender.

Slavko carried the letter into the kitchen and laid it on the table. He circled the table without sitting down to resume his breakfast and apparently with no imminent plan to open the letter. It was as if he was planning an ambush when the said letter was least expecting it. Suddenly he did just that, grabbing the letter from off the table and ripping the envelope open with no obvious regard to whether he might rip the contents within.

He unfolded the two sheets only to find that they too were typed. He quickly turned the last sheet over to discover what he had feared. The page ended without a signature or even an initial. The letter was anonymous. For a moment Slavko Nikolov was frightened to proceed further. He had little doubt that the letter concerned his wife, but what would it tell him and what was the motive of the writer? Was it benevolence or was it some kind of warning? Like everyone in the town he was aware of the letter recently received by Tatyana's uncle telling him his brother was dead. If this communication held a similar message he was not sure he would be able to bear it.

He sat looking at it for quite some time. He even resumed his breakfast as if the delivery had not actually taken place. He actively tried to forget about it, but the incriminating sheets of paper remained there on the table. At last he took up the letter and reaching for his spectacles began to read.

"Dear Slavko Nikolov,

It has become known to me that you have recently resumed your efforts to identify the whereabouts of your wife, Vesela. I understand this as her sudden disappearance must have been a shock to you, but I would caution you about continuing in this endeavour.

Vesela left of her own free will and is safe. She would want you to know that you were in no way to blame for her disappearance and that her decision to leave was not anything to do with matters between you and her. She says that she loved you and still does, but for reasons that cannot be explained she will not be returning to you now or in the future. You will never see her again.

While this news will be upsetting to you it should help you settle back into your current life in the knowledge that she is safe. Please heed my advice and give up your search which, given it will be fruitless, will only cause you more pain.

Yours,

A well-wisher"

Slavko Nikolov had such a mixture of emotions he struggled to even identify his own feelings and thoughts. There was anger there, of that there was no doubt. The sheer audacity of advising him against looking for his own wife was beyond arrogance. That such a person could then sign off as a well-wisher was outrageous. Briefly he considered that Vesela might have written it herself, but it was somehow clear to him that she could not have. He did not know how he was so certain about this, but he was. He felt relief that she was definitely alive. He knew this to be so, not because he believed what was written, but from the simple logic that he would not otherwise be told not to look for her. Whether she was safe, as the letter said, he had no idea. How could he know this when he had no clue who was telling him so?

His next thought was that the letter was a clumsy attempt at ending his search. There were no answers in the letter that would cause him to stop searching and equally the letter was not threatening, although he thought that maybe the writer intended it to be. Finally he wondered how the writer even knew he was looking for Vesela. In truth since the days and weeks following his discovery of Vesela's letter to her sister he had done very little. In his head he was still looking for her, but he had done nothing that would alert the outside world to his quest.

One thing was clear: she was out there. The only part of the letter that he would not dismiss was the claim that she loved him, that she still loved him. Ironically, the letter that was intended to warn him off was now spurring him on. Leaving the remnants of his breakfast on the table, Slavko took his jacket from the hook where it always hung and left the house. Now for the first time he had something tangible. The police inspector would have to listen and at last maybe do something.

As was usual, Slavko stood at the desk at the entrance to the police station for some time before anyone bothered to come forward to see what he wanted. When he asked if he could speak to the police inspector the officer became even less helpful.

"He is busy," he was told. "You will have to make do with me. Name?" Slavko was about to embark on what he knew would be a long and arduous battle to gain an audience with the Inspector when the man himself appeared in the doorway.

"Nikolov, what is it now?" he asked with a mixture of resignation and morbid fascination. The old teacher certainly had staying power, he thought to himself. "It's alright, Danchev, show him into my office."

Wordlessly the officer stood aside and allowed Slavko to enter. He waved in the general direction of the inspector's office and went back to whatever he had previously been doing.

Once sat in front of the inspector, Slavko launched straight into the reason for his visit. For the first time in years the tired and cynical policeman showed a modicum of interest. Slavko handed him the letter. The Inspector eyed it curiously and then began to read.

After reading it through a couple of times he lifted his head and looked at Slavko.

"And you say you have no idea who it is from?"

Slavko was clear. "I have not got the slightest inkling," he replied.

"Your wife perhaps?" the Inspector suggested.

"Absolutely not," said Slavko emphatically.

"How can you be so sure?" the Inspector continued.

"If you were in a situation like mine and you received a letter like that, would you not know whether it was from your wife?" Slavko asked the Inspector.

The Inspector thought for a moment. Unfortunately, he had not been lucky enough to have his wife disappear, but he took the point.

"Was your wife what you might call political?" the Inspector asked pursuing a new line of enquiry.

"Well, she had some strong views, like all of us, but no, I would not describe her like that."

The Inspector looked hard at Slavko. He did not like people with strong views. In his experience they were trouble.

"What are you saying?" the Inspector continued. "What views did she have? Was she some kind of agitator?"

Now the questions were getting ridiculous, but Slavko knew better than to be taken down this line. He became suddenly more cautious. "She was just a housewife," he replied. "Like me, she had no real interest in politics."

The Inspector let it go, but he would be careful to keep an eye on Nikolov from now on. You could never be too sure.

"We will look into it," said the Inspector indicating that the interview had come to an end. He folded the letter and was putting it into his desk drawer when Slavko objected.

"I want the letter back, please," he said. "It is the first news I have had about my wife in years."

The Inspector ignored his request and shut the drawer. "It is police evidence. Now if you don't mind I have things to attend to."

He stood up and knowing it was futile to complain Slavko walked out of the office, through the station and onto the street.

Back home Slavko sat with a glass of rakia in front of him and thought about all that had happened. He was angry with the police inspector, but also with himself that he had returned home without the letter. He should have insisted the police hand it back to him, but the truth was he had been afraid. He knew from bitter experience that the police were more than capable of turning the whole thing on its head if it suited them and he had no wish to spend another night in a police cell.

On the other hand the Inspector's questions about Vesela's politics had set him thinking. Out of fear he had described his wife as a housewife with no real interest in politics, but this was untrue on both counts. Although for the latter part of their life together she had not worked she was, like him, a teacher by profession. She had ostensibly given up her career in order to look after the house and garden and to better meet the needs of her husband. This is what she had said, but now he wondered. Her father had been a leading figure in the Bulgarian Agrarian National Union and she too had been sympathetic to their cause as well as showing support for the communists.

Slavko thought back to the last years that they were together recalling the numerous times that he got home to find that Vesela was not there. She always brushed off any queries from him about her whereabouts saying she had been visiting her sister, or had forgotten something at the shops and so on. For a short while he had feared she was having an affair, but never really believed this to be the case. Had he missed something? Political action was in her blood. Maybe she was more directly involved than he had realised.

He wondered to himself what the police would do now, if anything. Would they make any attempt to find Vesela and if they did find her what would become of her? If, as he now suspected she was a member of the Communist Party then she would possibly be arrested. How he regretted taking the letter to the police. If he was to keep Vesela safe he would need to find her first.

*

Now that he had made the decision to put thoughts of Tatyana behind him, Tsvetan threw himself wholeheartedly into university life. He enjoyed his studies and was an able and conscientious student. As time went on he became very excited at the idea of being a teacher and reported this sentiment to his old mentor in a series of letters. He would not forget that he had much to thank Slavko Nikolov for. What he did not know was that Slavko was supplementing the bursary that Tsvetan received from the school with his own savings.

Tsvetan came to love his life in Plovdiv and the longer he was there the less inclined he was to ever return to the small town where he was born. He made a lot of new friends mainly, but not entirely from amongst the student body. He dated two girls in his first year at Plovdiv, firstly a fellow student and later a local girl whom he met at church. The student, Nadya, was a member of the same seminar group as Tsvetan and he had at first noticed her because of the self confidence that she showed when speaking in the group. He envied this which was in marked contrast to himself. If Nadya had something to say she would just say it however raw and untutored the idea was. He on the other hand always felt the need to be on safe ground before expressing a view, even on subjects that he knew a lot about.

The girl from his church was the complete opposite of Nadya. She was extremely shy and unassuming. She was however very beautiful and Tsvetan felt guilty that he had been attracted by this alone. Milen would have laughed in his face at such stupidity. Neither of these relationships lasted very long and after a while the idea of having a girlfriend became less important to him.

For quite a long time Tsvetan attended services at both the Orthodox Church and the Catholic Church, but was aware that this was not entirely appropriate and sooner or later a choice needed to be made. In Tsvetan's view the Roman Catholic Church had the strongest intellectual tradition in Christianity and this mattered to him. The cultural tradition was equally deep and this too was a strong draw for him. He read the bible diligently and prayed to God for guidance and slowly he found himself moving closer in his mind to the teachings of the Catholic Church. Finally, after very careful consideration Tsvetan decided that he wanted to make a permanent move. He wrote immediately to the people who he felt should be consulted: his parents, Slavko Nikolov and Father Yosif.

Meanwhile the clouds of war had gathered in Europe and he was appalled to see that Bulgaria, along with neighbours Romania and Hungary, joined the Axis powers presided over by Germany, Italy and Japan. Tsvetan had both expected and feared this. He was unhappy with the actions of both the Roman Church and the Bulgarian Orthodox Church in response to these developments and for some time suffered a feeling of spiritual and moral disconnection. For a while he found more kindred spirits from amongst his college friends, most of whom were appalled by the fascism sweeping across Europe, than within the church and this troubled him.

Despite these reservations, when replies came from home giving him permission to follow his conscience, he formally became a Roman Catholic. As the Bulgarian economy suffered a decline he saw more support on the ground from the Catholic Church towards the Bulgarian people than from elsewhere and this lifted his spirits. With great enthusiasm and commitment Tsvetan engrossed himself in Catholic charitable work within the town. This was how he wanted to serve both God and the community in which he lived. By the end of the year he would be a qualified teacher and he was eager to take up the profession for which he had trained. However, the idea of eventually becoming a Catholic priest was never far away.

Chapter Twelve

Tsvetan's graduation in the summer of 1941 was a proud moment for him and his parents. His parents spent a considerable amount of their meagre savings making the trip to Plovdiv where they spent a magical day with their eldest son. With a mixture of pride and sadness Tsvetan learned that his little brother Grozdan had stayed at home to look after the smallholding and all the animals.

"He is a natural on the farm," their father had announced proudly. "We have come to rely on him a great deal." This was music to Tsvetan's ears as he had never completely forgiven himself for leaving his parents to manage without him. Thanks to his brother he could pursue his own ambitions without that nagging guilt.

Slavko Nikolov had written to Tsvetan to accept his invitation to the graduation, but in the event had sent a message with Tsvetan's parents to say he could not make it after all. This had mattered to Tsvetan and it frustrated him that his parents were unclear as to why his old teacher had not been able to come.

"He is certainly not unwell," his father had told him. "I am not sure what has prevented him from attending. Perhaps just another engagement?" he speculated. Tsvetan was worried although he did not know quite why. He and Slavko Nikolov had kept in touch throughout Tsvetan's time at Plovdiv and he knew that for the old teacher this was an important moment that he would want to share. Other than illness he could not think what would have caused him to stay at home. However, he was forced to put this to the back of his mind to ensure that he gave proper attention to his parents' visit.

As they sat in the university hall seeing their son graduate as a teacher, Tsvetan's parents had mixed emotions. As he walked onto the stage in his black gown and university sash to receive his degree their pride overflowed. His father puffed out his chest to the point that the buttons on his old suit, made for him when he was younger and slimmer, looked fit to burst. For his mother it was what she had always dreamed of. An intelligent woman, she was born into a time when such opportunities were not afforded to women and she had never anticipated it for herself. To see her son graduate was therefore the culmination of her highest hopes.

Good parents believe, in principle at least, that their sons and daughters should choose their own course, but it is nevertheless natural and not wrong for them to harbour hopes and dreams of their own. Tsvetan's parents had long since come to terms with the fact that he would not return to Svishtov other than as a visitor. They were pleased that with the clever encouragement of Slavko Nikolov he had chosen to be a teacher and they understood that such a vocation could take him anywhere.

However, they had always hoped that he would meet a young woman with whom he would have children and through that lead a fulfilling and happy life. Indeed his father had hoped that something would develop between Tsvetan and Tatyana, but the tragedy that had befallen that family had brought a premature end to any such notions. Tsvetan's parents were not fools. They knew where Tsvetan's decision to become a catholic was likely to eventually lead him and they very much regretted it. Nevertheless, if this was the path that he took in the future then they would support him. For now he had secured a teaching post right here in Plovdiv and that was to be celebrated. Above all they hoped that the uncertainties of war would not hinder their son's promising future.

*

Slavko had been looking forward to Tsvetan's graduation, but the day before he was due to leave for Plovdiv he had a visit from someone that turned his world inside out, but nevertheless left him with fresh hope. His visitor was Milen's father whom he knew only as well as a teacher would know any of their pupils' parents. It was well known throughout the town that Milen's father was a member of the Communist Party of Bulgaria. Although the party was still an officially banned organisation in Bulgaria, in small towns like Svishtov it was generally tolerated. Milen's father certainly made no secret of his membership. Milen had not been a pupil of Slavko for a number of years. In fact his own graduation from the local Academy was scheduled for later that month and Slavko was sure that the visit was not to discuss Milen in any way. Against all the odds he dared to hope it concerned his wife.

Slavko asked his guest into the kitchen. He offered coffee and then rakia, but both were declined. The man had a not unpleasant smell of fish on his clothes from which Slavko deduced that he had come directly from work. He came quickly to the point of his visit.

"I understand from my son that you remain interested in the whereabouts of your wife?" he said. Slavko had not spoken to Milen for at least two years so he could assume that he knew this from Tsvetan. Slavko confirmed that he would be glad to hear any news of her and so his guest continued. "It is not very much, I am afraid. I have not seen her and I have no idea where she is, but I have heard reports of her. I know her to be alive."

Slavko was sat bolt upright, shaking with tension and anxiety. "Please go on." he said in a low almost inaudible voice.

Milen's father hesitated. He could see the reaction he was causing and wanted to present what he had to say in a way that would not over-excite the vulnerable old teacher. He took a worn out, but freshly laundered handkerchief from his voluminous trouser pocket and blew his nose. "Excuse me." he said and clearing his throat continued.

"Did you know your wife is a member of the Bulgarian Communist Party?" he asked.

"I did not know for sure, but recently I had come to this conclusion," Slavko replied.

The fisherman carried on with his story. "As far as I can gather she is very senior in the party. Recently we were ordered to carry out a particular task which many of us were reluctant about. For obvious reasons, I cannot give you any detail. We were then told that the order came directly from Comrade Vesela Nikolova. At first this meant nothing to me, but I now understand that this is your wife's name."

At first Slavko Nikolov gave no response other than a slight nodding of the head. Milen's father looked on uncertainly. He had no idea how the old man was taking the news. Slavko's emotions were in total turmoil and he seemed for a moment to have lost the power of speech. He stood up and walked across to the stove where a metal coffee pot had been standing since lunchtime. Apparently forgetting that his guest had declined his offer of coffee he filled two mugs with the now treacle like brew. With his back to Milen's father he spoke.

"I am aware that your comrades would not approve of your visit to me and so I am doubly grateful to you. You need not worry, I will say nothing to anyone." Slavko then turned to look directly at the anxious face of the fisherman. "Do you have any information as to where the order came from? I mean do you have any sort of headquarters?"

"If I knew the answer to that I would not be able to tell you, but the honest truth is I do not know. The party has to be very careful."

"Of course, of course. You have been more than kind coming here at all. I will not question you anymore."

With that Slavko walked towards the door and Milen's father followed, relieved to be able to bring the discussion to an end. As he went out of the door into the overgrown garden he looked furtively left and right before quickly and silently getting on his way.

Left alone Slavko sat and considered this new piece of information. Had he during their marriage completely underestimated his wife? It appeared that she was not just a member of the Communist Party, as he had for some time suspected, but a leading figure, perhaps even the local commander. This now made sense. Although members of the party like Milen's father were tolerated by neighbours and largely ignored by the authorities, they would not ignore someone in a position of power. This did provide some credible explanation for Vesela's disappearance.

However, having acquired this information, what could he do with it? He was aware that should he try and involve someone like Milen's father he would be asking that person to take unacceptable risks. The backlash could come from the authorities or from within their own party. He now knew more than ever before about what could have happened, but was he any closer to finding her? Might he one day see his wife again? Slowly he was coming to the conclusion that this would only happen if she were to seek him out and this seemed no more likely now than before.

*

Tsvetan looked at himself in the mirror for the final time. His new suit, tie and shirt had cost him much more than he could readily afford. The local tailor had been kind enough to agree to him paying in two instalments and so at least he would not have to find the balance until after his first pay cheque. He wished that his mother could have been there to look him over, but he was reasonably confident that he looked alright for his first day as a teacher at the new secondary school.

He was very excited to be starting at a new school on the very day that it opened to new pupils. The school in Ivan Vazov Street was housed in an old building that had previously been the town's main police station. A lot of work had been carried out to convert it to its use as an education establishment, but some odd features remained that gave more than a clue as to the building's original identity. The most striking of these were the small individual study rooms that had either no windows at all or a small aperture high upon one wall, all too easily giving away that they had at one time been police cells.

Tsvetan said goodbye to Mrs Marinova who came out into the hall to wish him well. She did a reasonable impersonation of his mother by turning down the collar of his jacket more neatly and brushing away some non-existent specks of fluff.

"You look fine," she assured him. "Better than that, you look very handsome. If there are any young ladies on the staff they will be eating out of your hand by this evening."

She too was aware of his ambition to become a Catholic priest and had never seen him show any interest in young women, but she would continue to encourage him. He gave her a knowing smile. After sharing her house for several years they had become quite close.

"If I don't bring a young lady home on the first night, try not to be too disappointed," he joked and having got the better of her for once, left the house.

He arrived at the school forty minutes before he was expected and at first hovered about outside not wanting to either appear over keen nor to get under anybody's feet. However, after about ten minutes having observed others entering the building he decided it was alright to go in himself. As he passed through the new wrought iron gates it dawned on him what he had achieved from humble beginnings and also the sacrifices others had made to make it possible.

Chapter Thirteen

1943

Although Bulgaria had remained formally a member of the axis of power, the country had played little active part in the war resisting pressure from Germany to support the eastern front they had opened against the Soviet Union. Bulgaria's stubborn resistance to committing troops was very popular at home, where little enthusiasm for war existed. Nazi pressure to enforce anti-Jewish policies also had little support in Bulgarian society.

As a result, although Tsvetan remained opposed morally and intellectually to the actions of his country's allies he was never called upon to put this opposition on the line. He continued happily as a teacher in Plovdiv, doing a job that he really liked, but his desire to serve God as a Catholic minister was growing. Through its schools and libraries, its two large hospitals, one of them in Plovdiv, and its orphanages and old people's homes, the Catholic Church of Bulgaria was making a social, educational and cultural contribution out of all proportion to its size. This cemented Tsvetan's view that he had done the right thing by converting to Catholicism. However, opportunities to train to be a priest were few in Bulgaria with just a dozen or so teaching brothers trying to fulfil this role.

To advance his ambitions to become a priest Tsvetan knew he would have to study abroad. This would of course have advantages beyond receiving sound theological training. It would allow him to experience European culture and gain fluency in other languages. His problem had been the state of politics in Italy, his chosen destination, where the Fascists still held a tight grip on Italian society. However, when Mussolini was imprisoned, albeit by other members of the Fascist Party, he saw this as a sign that Italy was changing at last and that maybe his time had come. The first thing he did was consult with his own priest in Plovdiv with whom he already had a strong relationship. Father Antonov was very encouraging having for some time believed that Tsvetan had all the qualities to make an excellent priest. He also promised to do all he could to support Tsvetan were he to apply for a scholarship.

With his priest supporting him, Tsvetan's mind was made up. He first contacted his parents to tell them of his plan and then spoke to his Headmaster. Finally, Tsvetan submitted an application to the Roman Catholic Church for a scholarship to study in Italy and by the summer of 1943 he had been accepted.

*

Tsvetan and Milen had remained friends throughout the war although the opportunities to see each other were few and far between. Since graduating from the Dimitar Apostolov Tsenov Academy Milen had, to Tsvetan's surprise, started to forge a career as a government economist in the Veliko Tarnovo region. He was highly regarded and seen as having a bright future. However, the combined effects of studying Marxist economics and the influence of his father were having a profound effect on him and increasingly he found himself at odds with the prevailing attitudes within the Ministry of Finance and Economic Management where he was employed. By day he was a reliable public servant, but in his own time he was becoming politically active within the Bulgarian Communist Party.

When they did manage to get together their conversations were often quite difficult. Ironically, given how things had been in their youth, Milen was now cast as the radical with Tsvetan defending the age old role of the church. To Milen the church was at best an irrelevance and at worst a force for keeping people in their place. However, despite these fundamental differences their friendship remained as strong as ever.

It was therefore with considerable sadness that Milen received the news that his best friend was shortly to leave for Italy. There was some discussion between them about the current state of politics in Italy. They were now united in their loathing of fascism and both of them believed that the Fascists' hold on the country was weakening although they arrived at this conclusion from different perspectives. However, this was not now their priority. This discussion was for both of them a screen to hide the rawness of their emotions over their imminent parting of the ways. Although they both swore an oath to eternal friendship, they lived in an uncertain and rapidly changing world where shifting allegiances had the power to cut them off from each other. Although neither of them voiced their fears they both knew that they may never see each other again.

Tsvetan travelled by train from Plovdiv to Sofia where his parents and Milen met him to see him off on the next part of his journey into Greece. His beloved old teacher had not been able to make the trip as he was unwell and becoming increasingly frail. This added to the heartache Tsvetan was already experiencing about the imminent parting from his parents and his lifelong friend. Despite the sense of loss he was feeling he was also full of excitement and anticipation of his new life at the Italian seminary. He tried not to get upset knowing his mother would shed enough tears for all of them.

Strangely, once on the train and settled into his seat Tsvetan felt a growing calm. He was leaving all that he loved and heading for a dangerously unstable country, but these were not the things that mattered. After years of holding his plan to be a priest in check he was now on his way to fulfilling all his ambitions.

Tsvetan recalled the day on the boat when he had told Milen that he definitely wanted to become a catholic priest. Milen knew Tsvetan was in love with Tatyana and completely lost his temper over what he regarded as his friend's stupidity. Yet despite his feelings over Tsvetan's chosen path he had of course been there at the station to wish him well. Tsvetan recalled with shame the exact words he had spoken to Milen as the argument between them had raged: "Well for someone who's washing their hands of me you've got a lot to say for yourself. You should learn to mind your own business."

Tsvetan looked out of the window at the beautiful Bulgarian countryside, an expanse of forests and lakes dominated by the dome shaped Vitosha Mountain. Could anyone have a better friend, he asked himself. Tsvetan thanked God that Milen had not washed his hands of him after all.

*

Slavko was getting old. For all his efforts he had never found his wife or even heard from her since the day she disappeared. His sense was that she had never been far away, but that did not seem to make it any easier to find her. Now he was too old and frail to do anything about it. Although his time as a teacher had provided some rewards, he had spent much of his life alone and this he had never wanted nor planned for. Now that he was retired there was little for him. He had again fallen into neglecting proper meal times, a pattern that his young friend Tsvetan had temporarily rescued him from many years ago. He drank too much rakia and his doctor had told him that the rakia combined with a poor diet would do for him in the end if he did not change his ways. He had never found the motivation or strength of will to heed the doctor's warning.

Slavko remembered Tsvetan with affection and regretted he had not been well enough to wish him well as he embarked on the journey that was set to be his destiny. He thought back to the evening of the dinner invitation spent with Tsvetan's family. He felt some pride in how he had helped the young man and set him on course to fulfil his ambitions. For Slavko himself there was no such future now. The life he had led: that was it. He could feel that the doctor's predictions were soon to be realised and he no longer minded.

The following night Slavko lay alone in his bed having suffered a stroke. He could not move his body and felt himself going in and out of consciousness. As he lay there he was sure he heard a key turn in the lock. How could that be? The only person besides himself who had a key had not used it for nearly twenty years. The front door closed again and shortly afterwards Slavko heard familiar steps upon the stairs. Vesela stepped onto the landing and quietly opened the door to their room. Slavko was lying motionless on the bed that they had once shared. He managed somehow to raise his head and looked at her as a broad smile crossed her face.

"I am here," she said simply.

Chapter Fourteen

One minute Tsvetan would doze off and then suddenly with a jolt he would open his eyes and stare in front of him. Since the last time he had been awake the sun had gone down. In the moonlight he could see just about enough of the scenery and the architecture to tell him that he was now in Greece. A few minutes later, by way of confirmation the door of his compartment opened to reveal a Greek border guard. Tsvetan was the only passenger and had spread himself and his belongings across the six seats. The guard looked at him disapprovingly and he found himself gathering his things closer to him to make space although it was highly unlikely at this time of night that any new passengers would be joining him.

"Passport!" the guard barked. Tsvetan took the precious identification document from his jacket pocket and handed it to him. The guard looked from him to the passport and back to him, although the photograph had been taken only a month earlier and was an excellent likeness. "Where are you going?" the guard asked without curiosity.

"To Italy; I am catching a ferry from Patras," Tsvetan replied politely. The guard raised one eyebrow and Tsvetan found himself wondering how it was that some people could perform this gesture without the other eyebrow moving. He certainly could not do it.

"Why would you want to go to Italy? Do you not like Greece?" the guard inquired. The question seemed designed to intimidate Tsvetan rather than to elicit any information.

Tsvetan answered only the first part of the question. "I am going to a seminary to study to be a priest," he said.

"In my book there are already too many priests," the guard informed him. Again he compared the photograph in the passport with the young man sitting before him. Apparently satisfied he handed the document back to its owner and abruptly left, closing the door with a bang.

As the night progressed Tsvetan became increasingly uncomfortable in the poorly upholstered seat. He wished he had spent the extra money required to obtain a sleeping berth. However he was aware that the cost of this journey had already made a huge hole in his finances and it could not have been afforded. He had booked a room in Patras and would have to wait until then to get some proper sleep.

After almost twenty four hours the train pulled into Athens station, the final stop. As he disembarked Tsvetan was surprised to see so many passengers stepping from the train, not having seen a single soul during the journey. Perhaps he had slept more than he had realised or maybe everyone else aboard the train had been in the sleeper carriage.

Tsvetan had never been to Athens or to anywhere in Greece for that matter and had intended to spend some time looking around the famous and ancient city. However, a quick glance at the station clock told him that any sightseeing would be impossible. His train had arrived nearly two hours late and he had only twenty five minutes to locate the train to Patras and get himself and all his belongings on board.

The four hour train journey to Patras did nothing to remedy the fatigue he was now feeling. There were no proper seats or compartments except in first class. For the rest of the passengers there were just wooden benches and room to stand. Although he did manage to find a seat on one of the benches he felt obliged to give this up to an old woman as soon as the train started to fill up. For the first half of the journey he stood up, but like most of the passengers ended up sitting on the floor. When he saw the signs indicating that the train was pulling into the old port he felt a tremendous relief.

Although Patras was a large city he had booked a room close to where he would catch his ferry the following morning and it did not take him long to find it. The small suburban guest house looked very pleasant as he approached. On entering the foyer he was surprised to find that the pretty young woman who was employed to receive guests was anxious to find out if he was Tsvetan Viktorov.

"Yes, that is me. I have a room booked with breakfast," he assured her.

"Yes sir, your room is ready, but there is something else. I have a telegram for you." she told him earnestly.

Suddenly Tsvetan's stomach started performing somersaults. The only people that knew where he was staying were his parents. He feared bad news. Tsvetan did not have to speculate for very long. The young woman was anxious to unburden herself and soon thrust the telegram into his hand. With trembling fingers he opened the thin envelope and read,

> *Tsvetan stop your dear teacher Slavko Nikolov died in the night stop he did not suffer stop I am sorry to burden you on your journey stop mother with love stop end*

"Is there anything I can do, sir?" the young lady asked him. "Was it bad news, sir? I hate telegrams. They never bring good news. I am sorry, sir. Are you alright?" The colour had drained from Tsvetan's face and with one look at him the young woman could answer her own questions.

"Thank you for your trouble. I will be alright," Tsvetan said to her almost mechanically. "I would be grateful if you could show me to my room."

The girl burst into action, pleased to be able to do something practical. She attempted to gather up Tsvetan's cases in order to carry them to his room. Finding the task beyond her she left the largest case standing in the hall with a view to going back for it, only to trip over it as she attempted to reach the stairs. All the bags spilled onto the floor and the young woman fell headlong into Tsvetan's arms. She turned bright red and struggled to regain her composure. Eventually she stood upright again, but was further embarrassed when she realised she was still clinging on to her guest. So quickly and suddenly did she then let go of him it served only to draw attention to the fact that she had held on to him longer than was proper.

Despite everything Tsvetan found himself smiling and it was only from a sense of decency that he resisted laughing out loud.

"You must think me such a fool," she fretted and burst into tears. Tsvetan reached forward and held her shoulders which shuddered under his grip as the sobs shook her body.

"If you want to help me I could do with some company for dinner," he said, much to his own surprise. "What time are you free?" he inquired.

Her large brown eyes, round like a doll's, looked at him gratefully. "I finish at seven, sir," she said, quickly composing herself.

"That will be perfect. I will meet you here at seven. And please call me Tsvetan."

"Yes sir," she replied and bent again to make a second attempt at picking up his bags. He put his hand on her wrist.

"I will do that," he said gently. "Just show me where the room is." She headed for the stairs with Tsvetan following behind with the cases. As she went up the stairs in front of him Tsvetan could not help noticing that she had a particularly nice bottom.

Sitting in his room, Tsvetan did not know what to make of his own behaviour. On reading the telegram he had been desperately sad over the death of his mentor, but then within five minutes he was asking a pretty young girl out to dinner. At first he just wanted to save her from embarrassment, but thinking of it now he had to admit the pleasure he felt when she ended up in his arms. He was a normal young man with all the usual desires and it had been a long time since he had held a girl close to him. There was no reason to take himself to task. The news about his old friend Slavko Nikolov had hit him hard. He was feeling lonely and it was true that he could do with some company over dinner. The girl was pretty and certainly lively. He would enjoy his dinner date and think no more about it.

At just before seven Tsvetan went down to the reception area to meet the girl. He did not even know her name and would have to put that right as soon as he saw her. Tsvetan looked around him. There was nothing unusual about the small lobby. The walls of the room were painted a very light blue and the picture rail and skirting were white. There were a couple of paintings on the wall, by the look of them from a moderately talented local artist. There was an unlit cast iron stove of unremarkable design with a half full wood basket standing alongside. In the corner of the room with a direct view of the front door was a small desk behind which the girl had been standing when Tsvetan arrived.

The guest book lay open on the desk. To pass the time Tsvetan began idly reading through the comments left by previous visitors to the guest house. There were all the normal comments about comfortable beds, cosy rooms and excellent breakfasts which were reassuring, but of little interest. Of more interest were the comments about someone known as Avra. As many of these comments related to the warmth of the reception the guests had experienced, Tsvetan could deduce that this was the name of the girl he was now waiting for. He thought of the mischievous comments he could make from his earlier experience.

"The young lady received me warmly. She threw my bags onto the floor and fell into my arms." or "The receptionist was young and pretty and within two minutes of arriving I had invited her to dinner which she immediately accepted."

Tsvetan smiled to himself and seriously considered making just such an entry in the guest book. Just as he was deciding that he would write something Avra appeared before him. Tsvetan looked at her unaware that his mouth was hanging open. The girl was beautiful. Her ebony hair, previously up in a bun now flowed over her shoulders. She wore a simple sleeveless dress showing her slender tanned arms. She had used a little mascara to soften the roundness of her large dark brown eyes, but otherwise no make-up. She was as he would imagine a Greek Goddess making him feel fearful yet fascinated, in awe yet attracted.

"I am sorry I am a little late," she said. "I needed to get changed." As he said nothing in reply she continued, again feeling nervous in his company. "Where shall we go?" she asked then answered her own question. "At the end of this street there is a nice little restaurant, typically Greek. It is not expensive and no German soldiers go there."

At last Tsvetan regained the power of speech. "It sounds perfect," he stammered. Avra held out her arm and he took it in his and headed for the door, his legs still wobbly from the sight of her.

It was incredible how well they got on, talking without a break for what seemed like hours. During the evening Avra heard all about Tsvetan's life, his journey and his plans to join a seminary once he reached Italy. Avra found the last piece of information hard to understand.

"Why would a young good looking man like you want to take an oath of celibacy? It makes little sense to me," she told him and then rather unexpectedly she said, "Tell me about the girlfriends you have had. Have there been lots of them? Did one of them leave you broken-hearted?" Tsvetan found the question curious, but he realised the girl was still trying to find an explanation for his willingness to deny himself the love of a good woman.

"I have not had many girlfriends," he replied, "Only two or three and none of them were really serious. So no, I have not been hurt by a girl. My desire to be a priest is about serving God and the rest just goes with it." Tsvetan was determined not to count the only girl he had ever cared for amongst his list of girlfriends. It was after all little more than a fantasy. So he spoke of everything except Tatyana.

Avra had experienced the loss of her parents and her brother during the war, but had somehow remained optimistic about her own future. "My father and brother were both killed right at the beginning of the war trying to resist the Nazi invasion," Avra told him. "And only a few days later my mother attacked four German soldiers single handed and was shot."

Tsvetan gasped. "She must have been incredibly brave," he observed. He tried to appear calm, ready to support her if she broke down, but his fidgety fingers and his leg knocking rhythmically against the table gave him away.

"Not really," Avra replied. "She wanted to die. It was almost a suicide," she added.

Tsvetan was lost for words and just stared without speaking. In an attempt to lighten the mood before the evening was immersed in grief she decided to tease him.

"If you are going to be a priest you will have to improve your counselling skills," she said, smiling to indicate she was not serious, but she could not bring him round so easily and his mood remained solemn.

"It is all so tragic I am frightened to speak through fear of saying the wrong thing," he said, his face showing pain and real compassion. Avra took his hand, finding the need to comfort him rather than vice-versa.

"It is alright. I have learned to live with it," she said. "Sometimes I think they are the lucky ones. They were good people so I know they are together in heaven. It is me that is alone."

Then unexpectedly she gave him a broad smile. "But tonight I am not alone, so stop trying to be kind and let's enjoy the evening," she ordered. Tsvetan smiled back. In the company of such an infectious personality there was no other way. Avra finished her story. She had been grateful to the owner of the guest house, she told him, to provide her with a job and the chance to learn the trade. When the war was over she planned to open a hotel of her own with money left to her from her grandmother.

"Greece is beautiful. When the war is over there will be many visitors to our country," she maintained. "Not just those on their way to Italy," she added with a smile.

On their way back to the guest house where Avra had staff accommodation they held hands, laughing and pinching each other like two kids. Once back inside, standing in the small reception where they had met earlier that evening they were both reluctant to part. Avra was the first to speak.

"Tomorrow you will be gone and that will be it," she said with her face buried in his neck. "There is this terrible war. Greece is occupied by the Nazis and Italy is in the hands of the Fascists. Nothing is certain. By the end of next week we could both be dead. It is wrong to wait for anything."

Tsvetan pushed her gently away so he could see her face. "I am going to be a Catholic priest," he affirmed. "You know the vow I must take."

"I do," she said. "But you haven't taken it yet." He looked at her and temptation overwhelmed him. "My room is number seven," she told him. "Do what you think is right." Slowly, but gently she disengaged herself from his embrace and walked away.

Sitting on the bed in his room Tsvetan was in a terrible turmoil. He was a young man and she was a beautiful girl who had offered herself to him. Avra had opened the possibility of them making love in a totally matter of fact way. She was a girl who had lost so much she had taught herself to live in the moment. He was always preparing for the future, thinking what he would do in life, how he could serve others through God's work. But what about now?

Tsvetan thought back to when he was little more than a boy, fishing on the old boat with Milen in the late afternoon sunshine. Sometimes they would do reckless things like the time when they decided to dive into the water and race to the shore, although it was further than either of them had ever swam before. They made it, but only just. Tsvetan recalled how much water he had swallowed trying to keep afloat in the last twenty metres. Milen dragged him unceremoniously from the water, claiming the victory for himself. They sat there trying to catch their breath when they suddenly realised the boat was floating off downstream. Milen, always the bolder one, plunged in again and swam towards the fast disappearing boat. Tsvetan dived in behind him. If their neighbour Mr Dragov had not been there they would have lost the boat and possibly even their lives.

What had happened to that boy? He must still be in there somewhere. "You know the vow I must take," he had said to her, but to her in that moment it was not important. That could be dealt with another time. Outside Nazi soldiers strutted up and down in a city, a country that was not theirs. By morning the world could have changed. He stood up, walked out of the door of his room and went looking for room number seven.

*

The parcel boat that doubled as a passenger ferry was two hours out of Patras and the old port had disappeared from sight. All around was just open sea. The water was calm and the sun shone warmly down on the motley group of passengers, most of whom had no berth and were sat on the deck. The journey to Ancona would take more than twenty four hours and so the good weather was very welcome. Most of those on board sat in clusters chatting excitedly. Tsvetan, on the other hand sat somewhat apart deep in his own thoughts. He was asking himself if he had betrayed Tatyana, although he knew it was a ludicrous question. He had not seen her since he was just eighteen, but surely that was his fault. Milen would certainly say so. He wondered if she ever thought of him.

Chapter Fifteen

A thousand kilometres away Tatyana dragged herself home from work. She was exhausted. For three years now she had worked in a leather tanning factory in Sofia. The work was hard and the pay was poor. At first it had been particularly difficult as her mother was emotionally too frail to hold down a job and hers was the only regular money coming into the household. Since her mother's recovery they had at least been able to afford the rent of their small apartment and had enough money to feed and clothe themselves. Very occasionally they would visit a cheap restaurant on a Sunday and the two of them looked forward to these occasions as if it were Christmas. Her mother still had aspirations for herself and her daughter, but the necessity to support themselves following the death of Tatyana's father had pushed all ambition to one side.

Recently, however prospects had begun to improve. Her mother, Yordana, had for the last year worked in a clerical post at a large shoe manufacturer on the outskirts of the city. Then following the retirement of her predecessor she had become secretary to Cleto Rossi, the factory's owner, a job with a much better salary and prospects.

Rossi was only just forty, but had been widowed for four years following an accident in their factory in Italy that Rossi and his wife had run together. Following the accident Rossi had moved the factory to Bulgaria to try and make a new start. He had never before considered living and working elsewhere, but entering his old factory became a daily reminder of his wife's death that changed everything for him.

A business colleague had advised him to consider Eastern Europe to take advantage of cheaper labour and eventually he had taken the decision to move. Given the lack of trust between nations during the war years, the move had proven to be more complicated than he had envisaged. However, once established he continued to supply the Italian market, although now with a more competitive product. In the end Rossi did well from the war securing a lucrative contract to provide footwear for the Italian Army.

So from a business point of view things were going well, but at home there were difficulties. His mother had made the move with him in order to help with bringing up Rossi's two young children. After more than three years away from Italy she was feeling homesick and was also unwell.

"Cleto, I do not want to die in this Balkan backwater. I must return to Italy," she had recently announced. "You must find yourself a new wife."

Rossi agreed with her. He was ready to marry again, but he had not met anyone to compare with his first wife. Then out of nowhere Yordana appeared as his new secretary.

Although nearly ten years older than him, she was still a very handsome woman and he liked her a great deal. Yordana had a class about her that he greatly admired. Slowly he became fond of her in a way that he knew went beyond their relationship as boss and secretary. Unsure what to do next he spoke about her to his foreman and friend Geovanni. Geovanni had remained with his friend's company even when Cleto decided to up sticks and move everything to Bulgaria. They had been friends since boyhood and were very close, but they had a very different approach to women.

"You are right, Cleto. She is a very sexy woman. I have been thinking of trying to get her into bed myself," Geovanni confided. Cleto looked slightly aghast. He did not want Geovanni as a rival, but his friend had already read his thoughts. "Don't worry about me, Cleto," he chuckled. "I have enough on my plate with the beautiful Evangeliya. She is wearing me out. You make a play for Yordana. She is far too sophisticated for me anyway."

Cleto shock his head in disbelief. "I don't know why I asked you. I don't want to 'make a play for her' as you put it. I am thinking of marriage and a mother for my two boys, not some sleazy affair."

Geovanni's reply confirmed that asking him about marriage was indeed a waste of time. "Marriage is overrated," he announced. "Get your secretary into bed and find a nanny for your children. That is my advice."

Cleto went back to working it out for himself. The more time he spent with Yordana the more the marriage appealed to him. They enjoyed working together and he saw no reason why it would not work equally as well as a married couple. Also he knew some of his secretary's past life and assumed rightly that making ends meet without a husband could not have been easy. Surely he had something to offer in terms of making everything easier and more secure for her?

Cleto was also very keen to find someone who could grow to love his two boys who were precious to him. His mother had looked after them as only a grandmother can. She treasured them and although her decision to return to Italy was the right one she would miss them a great deal and the boys would be lost without her. His mind was made up. One day he found the courage he needed and proposed. For Yordana the proposal came out of the blue. She was completely taken aback. She had felt passionately about her deceased husband and could not imagine marrying a man who she did not love in the same way. She would have said no, but Rossi sensing this asked her to give more thought to the proposal before coming to a decision.

Without pressing her he talked with her about how life would be if they were together. Like many of his compatriots he was a good talker. Slowly his charm and persistence wore her down. She began to wonder why she had shown such resistance.

Yordana decided to tell Tatyana that she was considering marrying again and asked her what she thought. Tatyana was enthusiastic about the possibility of her mother remarrying. Since her own engagement in Plovdiv that her mother had virtually set up Tatyana always worried that her mother would again try to resolve their financial situation by finding a husband for her. This marriage would at least put an end to that.

"Mama, why are you asking me? Surely you know your own mind. You have told me many times what a lovely man he is. You are still young and beautiful. You deserve to be happy. Papa would want it too." Two months later Cleto and Yordana were married and Yordana and her daughter embarked on a new financially secure life.

For a long time Tatyana had not allowed herself to think about Tsvetan, but now with the freedom that comes with relative wealth she began to wonder where he was and what he was doing. She remembered that he always had ambitions to travel. She hoped he had been able to fulfil this ambition and speculated about where it might have taken him. She allowed herself this just for the pleasure of thinking about him. She had no plans to go looking for him or even to try and find out from his family or his friends where life had taken him, much as she would love to know. After all she had no reason to believe that he had the slightest interest in her. Quite probably, Tatyana told herself, he never gave her a thought.

*

Finally, Tsvetan's long and eventful journey came to an end in the beautiful Grand Duchy of Tuscany. His first sight of Seminario vescovile di Pistoia gave him a thrill that he had never experienced in his life. The seminary was built at the end of the eighteenth century. The pink stone buildings which included the church of Santa Chiara, formed a U shape around the lawn and garden. The buildings had a common façade of the simplest design and indeed simplicity was the defining characteristic of the seminary both inside and out. As Tsvetan stepped inside to be confronted by a long wide corridor with stone floors he felt as if his whole life had led to this moment. He felt sure he would be happy and that his long held ambitions to serve God would at last come to fruition.

He put down his bags to look around him and take in the atmosphere. As he stood there, his eyes trained upwards following the progress of a huge functional staircase, he heard someone address him.

"Tsvetan Viktorov?" the young priest inquired.

Tsvetan struggled from his reverie and attempted to give the priest his full attention. "Yes, Father. I am Tsvetan."

"Welcome, brother. We have been expecting you. I will take you to the rector, Father Spinelli. He likes to greet all new students."

"Thank you. That would be very kind," replied Tsvetan although inside he was trembling at the thought of meeting the rector. He had not expected this so soon.

The young priest led him, largely in silence, along the corridor and up the stairs that he had previously been admiring. They stopped in front of a plain oak door that stood open revealing a small simply adorned room. The rector sat behind an old desk reading.

Although not a particularly elderly man the rector was thin and bent, his gaunt face and sharp nose giving him the appearance of a bird of prey. He wore a pair of metal rimmed reading glasses low on his nose and looked at Tsvetan over his spectacles in a rather quizzical manner. Realising this must be the new student he stood up and came shuffling around the desk to greet Tsvetan with a conventional handshake. After a brief and somewhat stilted conversation he asked the young priest to show Tsvetan to his quarters and resumed his reading.

That night Tsvetan lay awake in the room that he shared with four other new students, one of whom was a young Bulgarian from Sofia. From him Tsvetan learned that during his journey the war had finally intruded into the lives of Bulgarians with a massive Allied air raid on Sofia.

With a new level of anxiety he thought of home, of his family and his friend Milen. He thought about Tatyana. Was she still in Sofia? He hoped that God would keep her safe. He also said a silent prayer for his recently deceased teacher, Slavko Nikolov. These were the people who had loomed large in his life, but they were all a long way from him now. He also thought about Avra. What had happened in Patras seemed to belong to another world. As the initial wonder of his arrival at the seminary subsided he felt a certain loneliness as if he was an orphan under the care of the Catholic Church. This was his family from now on. Only his God remained from his past life.

Chapter Sixteen

With great relief, Tatyana had given up her job at the tanning factory and was now seriously thinking about university. She had for a while assumed that she would attend the university in Sofia thereby remaining at home, but some aspects of her new home life did not entirely suit her. Over the last few years she had grown used to having her mother largely to herself and inevitably that had changed completely since the wedding. Secondly, much as she adored her two new brothers she was not wanting to spend long periods of time looking after them, as her mother seemed to expect.

In a weak moment she told the two boys that she might be leaving home soon and they immediately started wailing that they could not manage without her and could not bear it if she went away. She had been warned by her mother that Italians could be very emotional, but she had not expected it from two young children. It was only a matter of time until they blurted it all out and so Tatyana was forced into talking to her mother before she had time to prepare the ground. That evening she raised the matter with her mother and Cleto together.

"Sofia is a well-respected university," her mother stated emphatically. "Why would you want to go elsewhere? The education you would receive here would be far superior to anywhere else."

Tatyana could already see this was going to be difficult. She had never considered that help would come from Cleto.

"Superior to anywhere else *in Bulgaria,*" he corrected. "Why should Tatyana set her sights so low? You have money now, Yordana. She can go anywhere in the world."

Suddenly Tatyana was feeling excited. She had experienced only three places in her life and Svishtov alone had happy memories. She looked at her mother anxiously waiting for her response.

Yordana sensed it. "You have money, Cleto. I have none."

"If you want it that way: I have money and now I have a daughter and as her new stepfather I will happily pay for her education." Tatyana was open mouthed, but Cleto was not finished yet. "The answer is obvious: she should go to Italy, to Perugia, the town of my birth. It has a beautiful and ancient university and it is one of the best known cultural and artistic centres in Italy. Tatyana will love it there and they will love her, a beautiful woman in a beautiful city. It is perfect, Yordana."

"But is it safe there, Cleto?" Yordana asked anxiously. "There has been so much bombing in Italy."

"In the large cities in the North, but there has been very little bombing in Perugia and little damage. Although it is coming to an end, there is a war on, Yordana. Nowhere is safe, not even Sofia."

Yordana was feeling trapped. She was quite aware that Tatyana's head would already be spinning at the prospect, but she was fearful. In some ways she was surprised at herself and did not entirely understand her own anxiety. She had always hoped that her daughter would have opportunities in life that she had been denied both because her parents were never wealthy, but also because she was a woman. Suddenly she was being presented with an opportunity for her daughter beyond the wildest dreams of either of them. So why was she so resistant?

Twice in her life Yordana had made decisions on behalf of her family that had terrible consequences. She should never have dragged her husband and daughter to Plovdiv and having done so should have remained there after her husband's untimely death. Her parents and sisters would have given her all the support she and Tatyana needed. Instead she had fled like a refugee to Sofia where they almost ended up destitute. This time she must be measured in her decision making. In the past she had her husband as her rock, but now, God bless him, she was married to a man more excitable than her.

"I must think about it," she asserted. "It is very generous of you Cleto, but I need time to think."

"But, mama..."

"Hush child! I said I need time so please show some patience. For now the matter is closed." Tatyana was about to continue arguing her point, but a kindly look from Cleto advised her against it and she fell silent. Trying not to appear petulant she left the room. Her belief was that Cleto would be able to persuade her mother more easily than she might. Also, she knew her mother well. In the end she would not be able to resist the idea of her daughter living and studying in a place as exotic as Perugia. Tatyana went to bed happy that she was soon to embark on a new and exciting phase of her life.

*

In his first few months at the seminary in Pistoia Tsvetan worked diligently trying to integrate himself into his new life serving God. It was what he had wanted for himself, but in truth it did not always bring him the happiness he had anticipated. Despite being surrounded by others he often felt alone. Also the freedom and responsibility he had known as a teacher seemed to work against him. He was comfortable with the notion of subservience to the will of God, but struggled in an environment where the will of God was defined for him by others. He knew that he must find a way through this, but he was in essence an independent thinker. Surrendering this independence of mind was his biggest battle.

Outside of his daily struggles there were things to be optimistic about. The war was coming to an end and in Italy, much to Tsvetan's relief, things started to return to normal following the end of the Fascist nightmare that had engulfed the country. Although many Italians had been complicit in the former regime, there was no stomach for recrimination and with a few high profile exceptions these people merged back into their communities. Italy wanted to take its chance to move forward in a different direction.

Back in his homeland, a new nightmare was unfolding with the advent of Soviet sponsored communism. In Svishtov, despite all the political changes, his parents tried to carry on as before, but to his great sorrow Tsvetan learned that their land had been confiscated by the state and his father made to work on a state run farm. He heard nothing directly from Milen although he heard from several sources that Milen was now a prominent member of the Communist Party. Of further concern to Tsvetan was the persecution of Catholics. Bulgarian communists considered Catholicism to be the religion of fascism and Catholic priests were being charged with following Vatican orders to conduct anti-socialist activities.

Despite the massive dangers Tsvetan desperately wanted to visit his home to see for himself how his mother and father were managing. He had been away from Svishtov for a long time and as his life became further divorced from theirs he became increasingly guilty over how he felt he had neglected them.

Also he would dearly love to see Milen again. He had no fears regarding Milen's new position. The truth was they had never seen eye to eye politically even in their youth, but he was confident that their friendship would always prove to be bigger than any difference between them. However, he soon learned that the twenty or so Bulgarian seminarians studying in Italy, of which he was one, were being refused permission to return to Bulgaria. He longed to see his mother and father, but it seemed that for now he would have to make his future in Italy.

Chapter Seventeen

In time Tsvetan came to terms with his situation and settled down to life in the seminary. He always believed that his future would be as a Catholic priest in his homeland, but for now he would be content with whatever path God showed to him.

Following his ordination he was sent to serve as the priest in the small parish of San Martino in the village of Fognano, less than twenty kilometres from Pistoia. It was a workmanlike parish with a population of less than five hundred people who went about their business without undue fuss. They attended church; occasionally there was a funeral or a wedding to officiate at, but otherwise their call on the parish priest was minimal. He was aware that in other parishes in Italy the priest was central in the life of almost every family. That San Martino was not such a parish disappointed Tsvetan at first, but he tried to tell himself that God's ministry was of equal importance wherever it was performed. Tsvetan's problem was, and always would be, that he found this hard to accept.

*

Tsvetan had just completed his first six months as the priest at San Martino and had allowed himself a few days off from his parish duties. As he often had before he chose to use his free time visiting Florence, capital of Italy's Tuscany region, which was home to many masterpieces of Renaissance art and architecture. Tsvetan adored the city believing there were few places in the world that could rival its beauty. He had spent a wonderful day exploring the city, marvelling at the fact that every time he returned he found new sights to admire. As was his habit he ended the day with a visit to the Cathedral, Il Duomo di Firenze, for evening prayers. Tsvetan was now pleasantly tired and, although it was a lovely evening, he decided to take the bus back to his pensione rather than walk as was his usual habit.

Tsvetan was sitting on the bus in a window seat looking out at the passers-by. His lids were heavy with sleep and he was fighting to avoid dozing off. His stop was in less than ten minutes and he was frightened he would fall asleep and miss it. Although quite late, men were still working on the street that was being re-laid following the upgrading of the drainage system. The surface was being flattened by a massive steam roller that was making an almighty din, helping him to stay awake.

His eyes were drawn to a group of young female students most of whom had their hands dramatically held to their ears to shut out the noise from the roller. One amongst them, slightly older than her colleagues, was laughing at their skittishness. She seemed to hold herself apart as if she was with them, but not one of them. He was admiring her languid self-confidence when he realised it was a quality he had seen in her many years earlier. He was looking at Tatyana.

At the exact moment of recognition the bus stopped. Frantically he tried to get off, but standing passengers barred his way. He attempted to get past them, but suddenly realised he was going in the wrong direction. The door was behind him. As he spiralled round and pushed towards the door it shut in front of his face and the bus moved on. He crashed past people to get back to the window to see where she was. He saw her, now a hundred metres behind, but at least travelling in the same direction as the bus. Tsvetan made his way to the driver and demanded to get off, but the driver carried on.

"Calm down, Father," he advised, "We will be stopping soon enough."

Tsvetan desperately tried to explain himself to the mellow, unhurried driver, but his grasp of the Italian language failed him and he achieved nothing other than irritating the otherwise unflappable driver and some of the passengers around him.

They had travelled another four hundred metres before the bus finally pulled over and he had lost sight of her. Frantic now, Tsvetan leapt from the platform and began running back in the direction from which the bus had come, his eyes scanning the street for any sign of her. After a while panic set in and he lost any system to his searching, charging around in circles covering the same ground repeatedly. Finally, he leant against a wall exhausted and distraught.

He had lost her. He closed his eyes to try and prevent the tears that were welling up, but was unable to hold them back. He stood alone and wept.

"Father, are you alright?" a soft female voice inquired. Her Italian was more stilted than his, he thought. Tsvetan lifted his head to look at her, but his vision was temporarily blurred by the tears. Suddenly her voice became more urgent and she seemed to be speaking in his own tongue. "Tsvetan, is that you?"

Tsvetan had never expected this day to come. He had believed he would never see her again in this life and now here she was standing right by him in the middle of an Italian city.

"Tatyana," he said staring at her in disbelief. "I saw you and then you were gone and now like a miracle here you are." Helplessly he started to cry again, from relief or joy he was not sure. She smiled at him not quite understanding what he was telling her.

"I am not sure what you are saying, but I am no miracle, just flesh and blood. I live in Italy. I am a student in Perugia."

None of it made sense to Tsvetan, but he did not want an explanation. The sheer fact of her being there was enough. Without warning he took her in his arms and hugged her tightly.

"You have no idea," he said. "So much has happened. I tried. I tried to find you in Plovdiv, but your poor father. How could I have known?"

"Slow down, Tsvetan. I have much to tell you too, but one moment." Reluctantly she released herself from his grip. Suddenly for the first time Tsvetan realised that the group of students that he had seen Tatyana with were stood just a few metres away staring at the scene without any understanding of what they were witnessing. Their faces revealed a mixture of anxiety and curiosity. Tatyana approached them, said a few words and almost shooed them away like a gaggle of geese that she was wanting to lock up for the night. She returned and kissed him spontaneously. Neither of them knew the protocol for their sudden meeting, they only knew how they felt.

Arm in arm without speaking, they headed for a nearby café. As they went to sit down at an outside table they realised that the seating arrangements precluded further contact. Reluctantly they let go of each other and took their respective places on opposite sides of the table. Immediately they reached across the table but, somehow realising they needed to reign in their affection, placed their hands together in a gesture that identified them as friends rather than lovers.

"You are a priest," she stated as if he had forgotten or maybe never really knew before.

Tsvetan nodded. "Yes I was ordained here in Tuscany, in the Diocese of Pistoia. My parish is a short train journey from here." Slowly he was rediscovering his equilibrium, remembering who and what he was. Tatyana was still reluctant to make the same adjustment.

"Now you can never love me," she said suddenly, amazed at her own rashness.

Tsvetan was speechless. He was frightened to answer her fearing it would by necessity be some trite and banal response about loving all God's children. He did not want to disown what he himself was feeling nor ignore the truth of what she had honestly stated. Just as he was faltering his heart took over, taking control of his words.

"I could never *not* love you," he said and they each retreated into their own chaotic thoughts.

*

For Tsvetan and Tatyana alike, their friendship soon became the axis around which both their lives orbited. Whenever Tsvetan had some free time he and Tatyana arranged to meet. Sometimes they met in Florence and occasionally Tsvetan would make the trip to Perugia, a city that he also became fond of. However, without even really discussing it, they avoided seeing each other in Tsvetan's parish or even in his diocese. They did not believe they were doing anything wrong and Tsvetan had no intention of compromising his vow of celibacy, but people talk and he did not want to be the subject of that talk.

Wherever they were they tried to enjoy being together. At first even the simple things felt complicated. When they walked together they were unsure whether to hold hands. When they met after a long absence their greeting was sometimes very warm, but other times seemed quite contrived. In many ways Tatyana seemed more conscious of his status than Tsvetan himself and this sometimes caused her to behave in an ambivalent manner towards him. Occasionally he was surprised by her sudden irritation at something he said or did.

One beautiful day during their first summer together they were sitting on a bench in the park that surrounds the Villa Il Ventaglio in Florence. Casually Tsvetan put his arm around Tatyana and gently drew her towards him. To his surprise she pulled away from him and looked at him crossly.

"Don't do that. What will people think?" she said sharply.

"It does not matter what others think. It was an innocent enough gesture," he replied.

"Well if it does not matter, kiss me!" she retorted.

Tsvetan hesitated causing Tatyana to spring to her feet and turn on him angrily. "You see, it does matter. People can see you are a priest, so who do they think I am, some poor parishioner in need of your comfort?" For half an hour after that she would not speak to him and Tsvetan was at a loss what to do or say to put it right.

Over time they fashioned a way of being together that was similar to how a brother and sister might behave. Although their feelings towards each other did not bear any resemblance to a brother/sister relationship they made do with this set of arrangements. However, they both knew that in the long run their friendship was doomed to hit the rocks.

It was particularly difficult for Tatyana to continue like this. She was free to love Tsvetan and to be with him in the normal way. Indeed she had dreamt of just that even as an innocent seventeen year old. All the impediments to their being together lay with Tsvetan. She knew he loved her, but would he ever make a future possible for them? She would never ask him to give up his calling. If it were ever to happen it would have to be his decision alone. She needed to know his mind.

About a year after their chance meeting in Florence Tatyana decided she could not go on any longer. They were sitting in their favourite café in Via delle Streghe near the centre of Perugia. It had been a beautiful warm and sunny morning, but over the last half hour a cool wind had got up and storm clouds were forming in the sky above them.

"Shall we go inside?" suggested Tsvetan, but to his surprise Tatyana opted to stay where they were. It was as if the storm that was brewing was the appropriate backdrop for how she was feeling.

"Tsvetan, I am not going to ask you if you love me, because I know you do." He tried to interrupt to confirm his love, but she raised her hand, her palm pointing outwards in a gesture that said, 'hear me out'. "I know you love me, but will we ever be lovers?"

Tsvetan might have been shocked and surprised by the question, but in truth he had been expecting it for some time.

"Are you asking me to give up the priesthood?" he asked her, but she had no intention of taking responsibility for whatever happened next.

"I ask nothing of you other than to know your mind," she replied. "If you asked me to marry you I would do it tomorrow," she told him. "Will you ever ask me? It is a simple question."

Tsvetan felt trapped, not by Tatyana, but by his own lack of clarity throughout his adult life. If he had sought her out in Sofia all those years ago would his path have been different or would he have entered the priesthood anyway? He did not know. In the end he gave the only answer he could.

"I have made a holy vow to God. It cannot be undone."

This was what she had expected, but anticipating it did not make it any easier to bear. She sat and shed silent tears and as she did so the storm broke; the heavens opened and cried with her.

That evening Tatyana returned to her lodgings near the university knowing that she had to decide her own future from here. Her graduation ceremony was due to take place in only ten days' time and she would take that as her cue to return to Sofia. She would arrange to go to Florence to meet Tsvetan for the last time and tell him her plans. After the events of that evening he would be expecting it.

Tsvetan had booked a guest house for the night, but he had no wish to remain in Perugia a minute longer than necessary. He would take the train to Florence and stay the night there. In the morning he would return home. Sitting on the train to Florence he felt the most profound sadness he had ever experienced. It was almost more than he could bear. He thought back to those many boat trips with Milen when they had lived into the day gratefully taking whatever it offered. They had fished, talked about girls and thanked God, their parents and anyone who cared to listen for being those two young men there in the boat with their whole lives ahead of them. What had happened to his dreams? He was a Catholic priest in a parish that had little need for him, thousands of kilometres from home.

Chapter Eighteen

Cleto sat in his office with his head in his hands unable to fathom what had just happened. Out of a clear blue sky five security men had marched into his factory and arrested his wife for treason. For some time he had, as an Italian citizen, feared for his own position, but he could never have anticipated this. He had pleaded with the security men who showed only contempt. His foreman and friend Geovanni, who had moved to Bulgaria to remain as Cleto's right hand man, had tried to tell the guards they were making a mistake. A rifle butt to the face had ended his protests.

The factory had ground to a standstill as the workforce gathered around to tend to Geovanni and to try and comfort their kind-hearted boss. The terror was compounded for Cleto by the guards' refusal to even say where they were taking her. Suddenly he worried about his children. Might they be taken? It was irrational, but Cleto could not get this thought from his mind. Leaving his factory in a state of chaos and despair he headed for the boys' school.

Cleto had removed his boys from school with a minimum of explanation and was now on his way home, but he had one more task to perform. Somehow he must get the tragic news of her mother's arrest to Tatyana. It never occurred to him to keep this news from her in order to protect her. He loved Tatyana like his own daughter and this love was built as much as anything on mutual trust. She had to know. Cleto did not trust telegrams anymore. He was certain that a telegram sent to Italy would be intercepted and read. Not only would this bring more trouble down on them, it would most likely never be delivered. He would have to try and ring the university at Perugia to get a message to Tatyana, but how? The only person he knew with a private telephone was his neighbour and general practitioner, Dr Filipov. He did not know him well, but he seemed a decent man. He knew of no other option. He would have to trust that common humanity would prevail and the doctor would help him.

When Cleto arrived at the doctor's house with his children still in tow it was as if Dr Filipov and his wife had been expecting him. Cleto soon realised that the whole neighbourhood knew of his plight and his neighbour was eager to help. While Mrs Filipov looked after the boys the doctor took Cleto into the hall where the telephone was situated. With a gentle and supportive hand upon Cleto's shoulder Dr Filipov left him to make the call in private. Once through to the university Cleto's call was immediately transferred to the Vice-Chancellor. After a tirade about the scourge of Communism, the old academic assured Cleto that his message would be passed on as soon as Tatyana could be located.

Cleto ended the call and went back into the living room to thank his neighbours for their help.

"If there is anything we can do, just say," said Mrs Filipov. "They are such lovely boys. If you need someone to mind them for you it is not a problem. We are neighbours and in Bulgaria neighbours help each other."

Cleto thanked them both again. It was so kind and he was glad to find that neighbourliness, a trait that he associated with his homeland, seemed to be a universal quality. However for the time being he saw himself as the only person who could protect his family. He felt the need to keep his boys in his sight at all times.

Within ten minutes he was at home and was locking and barring the doors and shuttering the windows. That night he took the boys into his bed fearing for all of their lives. When he was sure they were asleep he quietly opened the top drawer of the small oak cabinet beside the bed. The Italian revolver was there with a box of ammunition beside it. He carefully picked up the gun and having loaded it, replaced it and shut the drawer again. Cleto never once closed his eyes. How could he sleep without knowing whether his wife was even alive?

*

Two days after her fateful afternoon at the café with Tsvetan, Tatyana was called to the Vice Chancellor's office. She had no idea what the summons could be about, but she went immediately to his secretary to make an appointment.

"Miss Kovacheva, thank you for coming so quickly," said the secretary. She was known for her warmth and normally she welcomed everyone with a broad smile. On this occasion her expression was unusually grave. "There is no need for an appointment," she added. "The Vice Chancellor will see you now. Please go in." All of a sudden Tatyana's anxiety levels went through the roof. She entered the room shaking.

"Sit down, my dear," the Vice Chancellor urged. "I am afraid I have some difficult news for you." Slowly Tatyana slipped into the chair opposite him. The colour drained from her face. She waited, expecting the worst.

"Last night I received a phone call from you stepfather, Signore Rossi. He told me that the Communists have arrested your mother."

Tatyana stared at him in shock and disbelief. "It is not possible," she replied unable to assimilate the information.

"I am sorry, but it is true," the Vice Chancellor told her. "According to your stepfather they came to his factory where she had been assisting him and arrested her on the grounds of espionage. She has been charged with treason."

At that moment the secretary entered without knocking, carrying two cups of strong coffee. "Drink this, Tatyana," she suggested. "It will help." Tatyana looked up at her as if she had no idea who the woman was. Mechanically she lifted the cup to her lips and drank.

"Is there anyone we can contact here in Perugia? A friend who can comfort you?" The Vice Chancellor's voice seemed to be coming from somewhere else, another room, another planet even. Tatyana looked at him blankly causing him to repeat the question. "Can we contact someone for you?" he asked. This time Tatyana seemed to hear him.

"My friend, Tsvetan, Father Viktorov," she said barely audible.

At once the secretary took up the request. "Your priest, that would be a great help to you," she said. "Where in Perugia is his parish?"

Tatyana smiled weakly at her, aware that she was trying her best to help. "His parish is near Pistoia," she replied. The secretary looked confused. "He is not my priest. He is my friend. I know him from home."

The Vice Chancellor looked knowingly at his secretary. He could see that the poor young woman would be in good hands.

"If you give Signora Armando the Father's details she will contact him." He stood as he spoke and offered his hand across the desk. "I am so sorry, but it will work out. I am sure it is all a terrible mistake." The Vice Chancellor kept his private thoughts to himself. He was sure it was a mistake, but that did not matter. If it suited them they would imprison her anyway.

In Signora Armando's little office Tatyana was getting distressed over the fact that there was no phone in the rectory at San Martino. However, one of the requirements of being a good secretary was resourcefulness.

"Do not fret. I will ring the post office in Fognano. They will find him and get him to ring me."

Tatyana nodded dumbly and then all of a sudden burst into tears. "Poor Tsvetan, what will he do?" she whimpered.

"He will come at once, I am sure," Signora Armando replied misunderstanding the question.

"I know he will come," she said tearfully, "But then, what will he do then?"

After speaking to the woman from Perugia University Tsvetan was quite clear what he needed to do. He contacted his bishop and told him he needed some leave to attend to a personal matter. The bishop was disgruntled about the request, but could tell his priest would take the leave anyway. Father Viktorov was one of his best and most reliable ministers. He granted the request. Within two hours of receiving the phone call he was on his way, not to Perugia, but to Florence. Several months earlier he had made friends with a rather dubious Bulgarian bar tender. Ivaylo had told him for the right fee he could get him anything. Tsvetan had laughed at the time.

"That is a strange offer to make to a priest," he had said, but Ivaylo was wiser than he appeared.

"You are a man as well as a priest," he had replied.

Tsvetan arrived in Florence and despite the cost took a taxi to the bar where Ivaylo worked. Thank goodness he was there. Tsvetan had no idea where he lived.

"I need a passport in someone else's name." Tsvetan told him without any preamble.

Ivaylo smiled. "For the priest or for the man?" he quipped.

Tsvetan took the joke at his expense on the chin. "I must admit I never expected to have to take you up on your offer, but I need to get back to Bulgaria and they won't allow me to re-enter because I am now a Catholic priest. So I must go as someone else. So yes, it is for the man."

Ivaylo smiled like a conspirator in a fictional plot. "Can I ask you, Father, is there a young lady involved?"

"Yes, there is, but…"

"No need to explain, Father," he assured him. "Ivaylo understands. The Italian women, they are irresistible are they not?"

Tsvetan resented the way this conversation was going, but perhaps he deserved it for being so pompous when Ivaylo had first offered his services. Ivaylo on the other hand was happy now. He did not like to think there was anybody who could resist the fall, particularly not a priest. Having had his fun at the Father's expense, he got down to business

"How good is your Italian? Is it at least good enough to fool a Greek or a Bulgarian?"

"I think it is good enough for that," replied Tsvetan hoping he was not overestimating his ability.

"Good, then you can travel as an Italian. There will be no problem at the Greek border. What happens when you get to Bulgaria you will know better than me. The only advice I can give is that you leave as much money in your passport as you can afford to lose. Then just hope that the Bulgarian border guard is greedy. Do you understand me?" he asked him finally.

"I think I understand you very well." Tsvetan replied.

Chapter Nineteen

"I do not understand what is bothering you, comrade," the young man said. "The woman is dispensable."

Milen looked at him with loathing. "The charges are ridiculous. The woman is no more a fascist than you or I. Anyway, she is originally from my village. I cannot just stand by and see her sentenced to life in a Labour camp when she has done nothing."

The young man felt contempt for his so-called comrade. "You say she has done nothing. That is the point. Too many people have done nothing except look after themselves. If the Party had not taken power we would still be living under fascism. Look at her. Instead of worrying about how she could serve her country the bitch marries a rich Italian so she can live like an aristocrat. My only regret is that her filthy husband was not arrested with her."

Milen could see he was wasting his time and also that this man could not be trusted. He needed to be careful.

"You make a fair point, comrade," he told him. "I will speak to Comrade Vesela about her. She will know what to do with this woman."

Vesela Nikolova had a lot of time for Milen. He was a bright young man and a committed Communist. Like her he was originally from Svishtov and had been a pupil of her husband. She had been watching his career with interest. When she was told he wanted to speak with her Vesela did not hesitate. Immediately she told her administrator to fix a time for them to meet.

"Comrade Milen. It is good to see you. Are you and your family well?" Vesela inquired.

"I am fine, thank you comrade. It is some time since I have seen my family but my mother keeps in touch. She says they are all well."

Milen was used to the more personable approach that was typical of Vesela Nikolova. Unlike most of their comrades she seemed to have retained her humanity. However, he knew he would need to be careful. She was also renowned as being quite ruthless when required.

"So what can I do for you?" she asked.

"You may know that a woman originally from our village, Yordana Rossi, has been arrested. You may know her as Yordana Kovacheva," replied Milen carefully.

"I know her as Yordana Rossi. She is married to an Italian" said Vesela sharply. "Why is she of interest to you?"

Milen was a little unnerved by the sudden change in tone. Vesela Nikolova may look like a benign elderly woman, but appearances were clearly misleading. She looked at him expectantly waiting for a reply.

"I have known the woman and her family since I was a child. I was surprised to learn that she was a spy. It seems so unlikely," he said.

Milen knew he was not handling this well, but he had to make some sort of stand. Like his father, he believed in the true values of Communism. Arresting and incarcerating innocent people did not fit with these values. Vesela was studying him hard. She was not going to make this easy for him.

"Comrade Milen," she began. "Unfortunately people surprise and disappoint us all the time. The Party must be ready to deal with such people, swiftly and harshly if necessary."

There was no point beating about the bush, Milen told himself. "Comrade Vesela, the simple matter is she is innocent of the charges," he said finally.

Vesela had not sat down again since getting up from her seat to greet Milen when he first he arrived. She walked slowly around the room, looking up at the two pictures that adorned her wall. One was a portrait of Georgi Dimitrov, the General Secretary of the Bulgarian Communist Party and the second one was an old print of Svishtov. Her eyes lingered on the painting of her home town for some time. Suddenly, as if making up her mind, she turned away from the picture to face Milen square on.

"How can you be so sure?" she asked him.

"It was my men who had to discharge the arrest warrant," he replied. "The charge sheet was a joke."

His frankness took her by surprise. "You are a bold young man, Comrade Milen," she said. Then after a brief pause she added, "Have her brought before me. I will speak to her."

"I am most grateful, Comrade Vesela," he said lowering his head to indicate his respect.

"So far," she replied, "You have nothing to be grateful for." She turned away and returned to her desk indicating the interview was at an end. With the faintest of goodbyes Milen quietly left the room.

*

When Cleto heard that his stepdaughter was on her way home he was surprised at how much comfort he derived from the news. For the first time he allowed himself to believe that the whole nightmare could somehow end. As an Italian he knew that people eyed him with suspicion. No doubt many of his neighbours believed that if Yordana had been involved in spying for the West then it would have been him that had put her up to it. Although he had been grateful for the help offered by his neighbours, Dr and Mrs Filipov, he felt completely isolated and impotent and the only true friend he had, Geovanni, was equally at sea. Irrationally, although she was still very young, he convinced himself that Tatyana would know what to do.

*

Disembarking from the ferry at the Greek port of Patras Tsvetan felt nervous. This was the first time he would be called upon to show his passport that identified him as an Italian citizen. In the event it went without a hitch, but he was aware that the real difficulties awaited him at the Greece-Bulgaria border. Once the anxiety of his first border crossing was behind him Tsvetan's thoughts inevitably turned to the young hotel receptionist, Avra, and what took place here in Patras a lifetime ago.

He had never spoken of it to Tatyana nor for that matter to any mortal soul. This was not because of guilt. Any guilt he carried had long since dissipated. He had told no one because it was something that happened between two young people who were afloat in a changing world, their moorings temporarily loosened. It was their memory and no one else's.

Tsvetan remembered with admiration Avra's positive attitude to life in spite of all that had happened to her and the terrible loss she had endured. In his mind he compared the course of his own life which in some ways was defined by self-inflicted repudiation of what he most desired. Avra had seen everyone that she loved taken from her. From that point on she had made herself a promise. She had no intention of denying herself any small pleasures that, in spite of everything, life conjured up for her.

Tsvetan had admired her, but had somehow learned nothing from her. He loved Tatyana and yet he had denied himself the ultimate expression of that love and to make matters worse he felt trapped in that denial. And yet what had he achieved so far in his chosen path as a Catholic priest? Nothing of note, he concluded. If he got safely back to Bulgaria then at least he must find a way of serving God and humanity that made his sacrifices worthwhile.

Tsvetan had often wondered if Avra had made it through the war and he thought about it deeply now. Irrationally he believed he might just bump into her, but of course that did not happen. He hoped with all his heart she had survived and if so wondered what she was doing and whether she was still in Patras. He hoped she had found some sort of lasting happiness and that she no longer felt herself to be alone. He dared also to wish for happiness for himself, although his life had never been more uncertain than it was now.

For reasons of safety Tsvetan and Tatyana had decided to travel at the same time, but separately. As a result they caught sight of each other from time to time without feeling able to speak to each other. Ivaylo, the provider of Tsvetan's fake passport, had advised this.

"There will be all sorts of questions for both of you," he had said. "It will only become more complicated if you are together." Tsvetan was committed to following this advice, but hung around near the port long enough for Tatyana to see him and at least know that he had come through the first passport check unscathed.

From Patras each of them boarded a train to Athens and from there to Kavala. They then changed train several times criss-crossing past each other until they eventually disembarked at the small town of Dimari. From there they had a long and anxious wait until the bus arrived that would take them to the border crossing near the Bulgarian village of Chepintsi. Ignoring each other was now getting particularly difficult as there were only nine people on the bus and two of those were Greek border guards.

From where the bus dropped them there was a two kilometre walk for the seven remaining passengers. Tsvetan's heart was thumping in his chest whilst Tatyana was suffering acute nausea that got worse with each step she took. Before leaving Italy Tsvetan had sent just one message home to inform his parents that he was on his way. Now as he approached the border carrying an Italian passport he bitterly regretted his folly. What if his mother had spoken about it to friends or neighbours? He did not know how aware she was of the dangers of travelling into Bulgaria. Perhaps the authorities would be waiting for him.

For the first time since leaving Italy he took a long hard look at the woman he loved but could never have. Even after the long and arduous journey she still looked lovely. Despite the anxiety and fatigue Tatyana held her slim body erect and moved with charm and grace. She was a joy to behold. He feasted his eyes on her aware that after today he might never see her again.

Tatyana, in her anxiety to get it over with was the first of the group to reach the border gate. One of the border guards looked her up and down making lewd remarks to his comrade. Tsvetan clenched his fists together and closed his jaw tightly to try and prevent himself from doing anything that he would regret. He was fourth in line and could see her shoulders shaking uncontrollably. He bowed his head and prayed.

The questioning of Tatyana seemed to go on and on. Whereas he could clearly hear the questions being asked, Tatyana's replies were barely audible and he could not make out what she was saying. The guard that had spoken so rudely about her was starting to enjoy her suffering. He stroked her face causing an involuntary shudder to go through her body. Then as he leered at her making a suggestive remark she lost control.

"Get off me!" she yelled. "Leave me alone." He took hold of her hair and just as Tsvetan was about to condemn them both to death through his actions a voice rang out from behind the border gate.

"Corporal, what do you think you are doing? If you want a whore go to the gypsy quarter in the village. Leave decent Bulgarian women alone."

The border guard swung round to confront the owner of this unfamiliar voice. He found himself face to face with a senior member of the notorious State Security Forces. Milen gave him a hard stare.

"We have an arrest warrant for this woman and for him," Milen decreed pointing his finger at Tsvetan. "They are together. Surely even an imbecile like you can see that?" The border guard squirmed.

"I had my suspicions," he lied.

Milen sneered at him. "I will speak to your commanding officer. We will have you back picking potatoes by the end of the week. You are clearly unfit for this task."

The guard held his tongue. So far he had not been asked to identify himself. If he was lucky the State Security Officer would forget the incident or just not be bothered. Milen pointed a gun at Tsvetan and Tatyana and ordered them to accompany him. Then before leaving with his prisoners he turned to the Corporal and demanded his name and number.

Now sitting safely in the back of Milen's car, Tatyana cried with relief. Tsvetan sat beside her dumbstruck. He was in awe of what his friend had risked for them. He tried to thank him, but Milen was still intent on completing his rescue mission. He needed to stay focused or all three of them were as good as dead.

"I will drop you both in Rudozem. It is a quiet town, but do not resume your identity as a priest. Things have changed here in Bulgaria, Tsvetan. Churchmen no longer command respect. Once you are in the town you are on your own."

Within ten minutes they found themselves standing by the roadside on the outskirts of Rudozem. Less than a hundred metres away was the Chepinska River. On the far side the river bank was lined by fir trees, but on the near side a rough path was easily visible. Milen had told them that if they followed the river they would soon arrive in the centre of town. Milen's car was disappearing into the distance. Shyly Tatyana took Tsvetan's hand. She had craved physical contact with him throughout their long ordeal. Tsvetan looked at her smiling and squeezed her hand in his.

"I think we both deserve a drink," he said.

Chapter Twenty

Yordana was a broken woman as she sat alone in her cell in the Belene Island Labour Camp. The cell was filthy and stank of urine. Her hair had been shaven and she had been deprived of sleep. They kept insisting that she must tell them everything: all her contacts in Italy, her accomplices in Bulgaria and what information she had passed on. She was not a brave woman. If she had known any of the things that they asked her she would gladly have told them. She would have given them any information that they required, but she was more in the dark than her interrogators. As night fell she wondered when they would come for her again. It would not be long.

Surprisingly dawn arrived and she had still not been taken again for questioning. As she waited she became increasingly edgy. She was starving hungry, but she had been without food for so long she doubted she would be able to keep anything down. Now that morning had come and light was streaming through the window high up on the outside wall of her cell, the strong lamp that had been burning her eyes all night at last went out. Soon she heard footsteps in the corridor outside her cell. She braced herself for whatever was planned for her. For a moment she hoped it was time for her execution, but once she realised this was not to be the moment of her death the relief was palpable. She still, despite everything clung to life.

Her door opened and to her amazement the guard handed her some bread and cheese and a glass of water. She wolfed it down not caring whether it would make her sick, but to her surprise the food stayed down after all.

"I am to take you to meet Comrade Vesela Nikolova," the guard told her. "You are lucky. She seems to be in a good mood today. Perhaps she plans to take you to lunch?" The guard laughed out loud at her own joke. Then reverting to type she poked Yordana hard in the ribs causing her to wince slightly. "Come on, Mrs Rossi. You don't want to keep her waiting."

The name of the woman that now sat behind the desk meant nothing to Yordana. She had no idea that Vesela Nikolova was from the same town in which she had lived for most of her married life or that the woman's husband had once been her daughter's teacher. To her Vesela Nikolova was simply a powerful officer of the Communist Party. Yordana was shaking uncontrollably. Her jaw was tense through anxiety and she could hear her own teeth chattering, but was powerless to stop them.

"Mrs Rossi," the woman began, "There is something you can do for me."

*

Yordana could not quite take it in. One minute she was sat in a filthy cell in the notorious Belene Island Camp and now here she was, less than a fortnight since her meeting with Vesela Nikolova, standing on the Bulgarian mainland close to the little town of Svishtov that she probably should never have left. She felt the top of her head where thankfully some hair was at last growing back. Although her own clothes had been returned to her she had lost so much weight in the camp that they hung on her like washing on a clothes horse. The release was so sudden she felt completely disorientated. She was aware that her face was dirty and her hands and feet were absolutely filthy. Although she had been given a travel warrant to get the train back to Sofia, if she turned up at the station looking like this she might be re-arrested on charges of vagrancy.

Suddenly Yordana had an idea. She walked along the bank of the Danube for about half a mile until she found a secluded spot. She then undressed, discarded her soiled underwear under a bush and plunged into the water. When she had washed herself as well as possible and had rid her body of the stench of her cell she clambered back onto the bank and dressed herself as best she could discarding everything except her dress and shoes. She hardly looked like a wealthy woman of business, but she could at least now show herself in public.

As she started the walk to the local station to catch her train home she tried to blank out the details of her discussion with Vesela Nikolova. Her release had come at a price, but at least she was free.

She would return home to her husband and try to take up the reigns of her life, a life that only a week earlier she was sure she would lose.

*

Now that he was home Tsvetan had every intention of continuing God's ministry, but he needed some time to work out how he could best serve. After the trauma of re-entering his homeland it was clear to him that returning to Italy was an impossibility. He wrote immediately to his Bishop apologising and resigning his parish. Tsvetan soon discovered that the Catholic Church in Bulgaria had all but been destroyed. There was in effect no hierarchy to guide him, but there were still pockets of Catholics all around Bulgaria who urgently needed God's guidance through the ministry of a priest.

Seeing his parents again was like a gift from God. Thankfully they were both well and, although his father complained about the inefficiency of the state run farm his daily life of farming and some fishing and had not changed significantly. Tsvetan did note with some amusement that, despite his father's entitlement to free vegetables as part payment for his work on the communal farm, he had converted their front garden into a vegetable patch where he toiled every weekend.

His mother talked incessantly, something he took as a sign of her continuing good health, and dragged every last piece of information out of him about his life in Italy. She showed him an old pre-war guide book about walking in Tuscany as evidence that she had been showing an interest in his new life. Her joy at having him home was diluted by her anxiety over his plans to give Catholic masses in Bulgaria. She told him how dangerous this could be although he was clearly aware of this himself. In the end she just let him be, deciding to try and enjoy whatever time they would have together.

Before leaving Svishtov to go to Sofia, which was his intention, he dearly wished to go out on the boat with Milen as they had so often done as young men when the world seemed a simpler place. Although Milen did come home briefly to see his old friend, he was reluctant to do as Tsvetan wanted.

"Believe me, Tsvetan, if you take the course you are planning there will be times in the future when you need my help. The more distance there is between us the better I will be able to help you when the time comes."

Tsvetan thought about this and wondered how Milen squared the circle between his common decency and the terrible things being done in the name of his Party.

"So despite our differences you would help me again?" Tsvetan asked him.

Milen looked at him harshly. The question, given recent events was surely unnecessary. "We are friends, are we not?" he replied.

*

Cleto was waiting for her at Sofia station. Tatyana could see him standing at the barrier as she alighted from the train. Even from this distance he was easily identified as an Italian, so different in appearance to the Balkan men surrounding him. An Italian man's face tells his story and Tatyana could see by looking at him that Cleto had news to impart, better news.

As she passed through the barrier he pushed his way forward, his face breaking out into a broad smile.

"She is home, Tatyana. Your mother is home."

They took the tram. The sound of it rattling along the street and the general hubbub of chat between the passengers made it difficult to have any sort of conversation, but as soon as they got off for the short walk to the house Cleto turned to her with an earnest expression.

"You must be prepared for a shock, Bella Mia. Your mother has changed since her time in the camp."

Concern spread across Tatyana's face. "What have they done to her?" she demanded.

"I don't know. She won't say. She won't talk about the camp at all, but I believe that terrible things have happened there. She is frightened to go out. That is why she did not come to the station to meet you. She won't entertain the idea of going to the factory. That is where they arrested her. It was the worst day of our lives." His lip started to tremble and he could not hold back the tears. Tatyana turned to him and hugged him there on the street.

He continued through the tears. "Your mother has changed towards me too. I am so happy she is back home, but she is sharp with me as if she no longer loves me."

Tatyana tried to remain strong. "Of course she loves you. You just need to give it time."

Cleto said nothing for a moment still worrying that Tatyana had no idea what awaited her. He made an effort to be more positive.

"She is so excited that you have come home, Tanya. I am hoping it will be the thing that brings her back."

Tatyana loved this man who had never tried to replace her real father, but that was how she regarded him. She held him gently at arm's length and he allowed his grief to take hold of him. She looked into his eyes, still dazzling despite the tears.

"Cleto, she is home. Between us we will find a way to help her. In time she will be herself again. You will see." At last Cleto managed to smile although the tears had not really stopped.

"Yes Tanya. Together we will do it."

Chapter Twenty One

It was six months before Tatyana felt her mother could manage without her. Yordana had by no means gone back to her old self, but she was stronger now, physically and emotionally. She had put on a little weight and her hair had grown long enough for her to wear it in a sort of bob. Her good looks were slowly returning and Tatyana had started to realise how much her mother's beauty contributed to her self-image and her self-confidence. She wondered if it were the same for her.

Tsvetan in the meantime had settled in a small village just outside Sofia. Tatyana continued to see him whenever she could, but as time moved on it became increasingly dangerous for Tsvetan to come into the city as the government continued their attacks against the Catholic Church. Most priests were killed, jailed or sent to Belene Island from where they never returned. Ordinary Catholics were constantly harassed and had few legal rights. Tsvetan eventually became involved with small groups of Catholic dissidents and continued to hold masses although this put his life at risk.

With her mother now managing reasonably well thanks to the love and attention of her husband, Tatyana made the decision to join Tsvetan and his small band of devoted Catholic followers. As a result of continued rapid industrialisation many of the small villages were abandoned as the rural poor were forced into the cities in order to find work. These 'ghost' villages provided a relatively safe haven for Tsvetan, Tatyana and others who had attached themselves to the now infamous priest.

By moving around it became difficult for the authorities to know what Tsvetan and his followers were engaged in or even to keep any track of where they were. Tatyana's role in the whole business was hard to define. Tsvetan had convinced himself that his vows of celibacy and obedience to God were not compromised by her presence. For her it amounted to belief in what he was doing and her overwhelming need to be near him. The conversation they had in Perugia at the café in Via delle Streghe seemed to be forgotten. Tatyana was resigned to the fact that Tsvetan would never disavow his promises to God and the Catholic Church. She had come to terms with the fact that they would never be lovers, but she realised that she could not live without him in her life.

Every day Tatyana feared it might be their last together. She was continually on edge and found sleep difficult even though she was often exhausted. Her mother, as she recovered yet further, became increasingly strident in her opposition to her daughter's way of life and to her relationship with Tsvetan, comprising an arrangement that she completely failed to understand. Tsvetan did not fear the end. He knew that it would come. He would face it when it did.

They both woke at the same moment. There was a ferocious knocking on the front door. A dog was barking. They knocked again. Tatyana appeared in Tsvetan's bedroom like a spectre.

"Tsvetan, they have found us. We must run."

Tsvetan was slowly pulling on his trousers. He was calm. "We cannot run. It is impossible to get away. We have done nothing. We will let them in," he said, taking control.

"I am frightened," she told him.

"I am frightened too, but we must be strong. We are not criminals. Only God can judge us."

"What good is God?" she blurted out. "Why does he not protect us?"

"He will. Now please stay here and stay silent. It is me they want," said Tsvetan emphatically.

Now fully dressed he went to open the door, fearing the old hinges would otherwise give way. "I am coming!" he yelled above the din. The banging stopped.

Tatyana admired his faith that never seemed to falter. She understood it was this that defined him. She on the other hand was defined by her hopeless love for him. She had no room in her heart for God. God had done nothing for her other than take away the man she loved. She sat on the bed with Tsvetan's old fashioned nightshirt pressed to her face. She covered her ears straining to resist her desire to run at them as they entered and claw at their faces. She would do as he had said. She would do it through love and obedience, but also because she was afraid. Her mother had seen the inside of Belene Island and come home a broken woman. She could not go there.

As Tsvetan opened the door four members of the security forces entered the dilapidated old house. The floor boards creaked threatening to give way under the pressure of stamping boots. One of the men lifted his hand with the intention of striking Tsvetan where he stood, but his superior officer put out his arm to prevent it, cursing the man as he did so.

"Show some respect. The father will come peaceably, I think."

Tsvetan looked at him in a way that despite the ridiculous odds gave the authority to him.

"I have done nothing outside the law, but if you require it I will come with you. There is no need for violence. We all stand under the judgement of God."

The barrel chested man who had intended to strike Tsvetan fell silent. He hated priests, but still from his childhood he feared their power.

The officer spoke politely to him. "Are you alone, Father?" he asked him.

"I am a priest. I live only with God."

From the bedroom Tatyana stifled her sobs with the nightshirt. She cried out of fear and pity for him, but also from the realisation that he meant the words he had just spoken. The officer stood aside and with a wave of his hand invited Tsvetan to step out into the night.

"Should we not search the house, sir?" one of the security guards asked.

"We came for Father Viktorov," the officer replied. "I believe this is him."

Tsvetan had expected to be arrested at some time. He was aware that although nominal official toleration of Catholic worship remained, priests were continually being arrested and charged with a variety of trumped up espionage offences. He had continued to hold mass for his small band of Catholics in and around Sofia and had not attempted to hide this from the authorities. He also taught without a salary in a small Catholic primary school that had been stripped of its official status and with it most of its funding. He therefore lived his life under constant threat of arrest. He feared this not for himself, but because for the first time he believed his work to be valuable and did not want his small flock and his young scholars to be deprived of God's ministry.

*

Tsvetan languished in prison in Sofia for more than three months with no explanation for his imprisonment. Eventually he was charged by the Ministry of Public Security with working for Western intelligence agencies and collecting political, economic, and military intelligence for the West. He soon learned that sixty other Catholic priests had the same charge levelled against them. The authorities required each of them to confess to their involvement. As a warning the first four who refused to do so, even under torture, were executed. None of the sixty priests were guilty of the ridiculous charges and whether they signed a confession or not had little effect on the outcome: they were tried and found guilty and either executed or incarcerated in the notorious labour camp on Belene Island.

The trials were a key element in the subsequent wave of repressions against the Church. The property of Catholic parishes was confiscated, all Catholic schools, colleges, and clubs were closed, and the Catholic Church was deprived of its legal status.

*

"It makes me so sad, Cleto," said Yordana putting down her coffee cup for a minute. "It was bad enough that she met up with him again in Italy when he was already a priest, but now she frets over him languishing in prison. There is no future for her with this man. Firstly he is married to the church and secondly he will probably die on Belene Island. Most inmates do, whatever the length of their sentence."

Her husband looked at her indulgently. In truth he had much more sympathy for Tatyana than her mother appeared to have.

"They released you, Yordana. So some people come home, thank God."

Yordana did not like to talk about her release from the camp. It made her feel guilty. "I was innocent of the charges. They knew that," she said.

"Father Viktorov is innocent I am sure," replied Cleto. "And I am equally sure that the authorities know that too. All the priests convicted of these absurd charges are no doubt innocent and now honest Catholics like me have to live their lives as a lie with no opportunity to attend mass. It is intolerable."

Yordana said nothing further. It was starting to irritate her that her husband was so sympathetic with regard to Tsvetan and even a little in awe of him. He had wrecked her daughter's life. She was glad he was no longer around. Maybe Tatyana would at last come to her senses. Cleto looked across the room at her almost as if he could read her mind.

"The simple matter is she loves him and if you ask me…"

"I am not asking you," she interrupted sternly, but Cleto was not to be stopped.

"If you ask me," he continued, "She will never stop loving him. You might as well get used to it."

Chapter Twenty Two

Tsvetan was riding in the back of an old pickup with seven other prisoners. They were all chained together and also to the side of the vehicle. An armed guard sat with them and three other guards sat in the cab in front. Escape was impossible, but even if it had been worth an attempt these were men who had been starved and tortured in order to drag meaningless confessions from them. They were bowed and broken. Some of them carried serious injuries that had never been attended to. The only thing that could not and had not been taken from them was their faith in God. All eight of the prisoners were Catholic priests.

They all knew where they were going and they all expected it to be their final destination on this earth. No one had ever escaped from Belene Island Labour Camp and only a handful had ever been released. To all the others the drive across the new bridge was taking them to a form of hell on earth. Only Tsvetan had ever set eyes on the infamous island before and his wonderful memories of the times he had shared there with Milen expunged the blackness associated with the island on this darkest of days.

As they drove off the bridge onto the island he could hear the familiar sound of the many different species of birds as their songs filled the air. In his mind's eye he could see two young men stretched out on the banks of the river Danube that they had just crossed in their old boat. Each held a bottle of beer in his hand. He recalled with a sense of irony the words spoken by his friend, unusually poetic for Milen:

"Wherever you go, Tsvetan, and for however long you will surely miss this place."

Tsvetan smiled to himself, a gesture that his companions, neither prisoners nor guards, could comprehend. Almost unaware that he was speaking aloud he repeated the words that he had said in reply to Milen a lifetime ago. "I will miss this place and this moment and many moments of friendship just like it."

Tsvetan lowered his head and found himself staring at the feet of his fellow prisoners. A tear fell onto the worn out shoe of the man next to him in the chain gang as the rickety old pickup clattered along the road towards the camp.

Tsvetan and one other priest had not confessed their crime and so as their colleagues were taken to their dormitories Tsvetan and the other hapless priest were put in a filthy, dilapidated room to await further interrogation. There was no furniture in the room, not even a wooden bench and so for nearly six hours they sat on the floor unaware of what to expect. There was no toilet and they were given no food or water. In fact no one appeared. Slowly it got dark and Tsvetan found himself drifting in and out of sleep. Suddenly the door opened and his colleague was dragged from the room. Immediately the door closed behind them leaving Tsvetan alone.

Tsvetan lay on the floor for another four hours before the door opened again. He was told to get to his feet and was then led to a shabby building and pushed inside. There he joined the other priests with whom he had been transported. The one who had briefly shared the room with him was not there and Tsvetan never saw or heard of him again.

Life in the labour camp was an endless pattern of exhaustion, suffering and sheer terror. Torture, rape, harsh punishment and death were part of everyday life. Although none of the wardens treated the prisoners with any humanity some were especially feared as they were capable of sudden unexpected acts of violence with their victims often suffering acute injuries. Like all inmates Tsvetan tried hard not to upset these particular wardens, but sometimes it made no difference and he too was from time to time the victim of unprovoked gratuitous violence. Medical care was non-existent and it was not uncommon for inmates to die as a result of neglected injuries that resulted in heavy blood loss or infection.

Each day the inmates were divided into small groups and given a work schedule for the day. Much of the work consisted of building cellblocks for further inmates as the numbers on the island were growing daily. They were required to carry out these building tasks with whatever materials they could find and with only the most primitive tools. They worked all day under armed guard without food. Everyone who did not accomplish their allotted daily work was badly beaten. Hunger was the most terrible thing they were subjected to. The food they did receive was disgusting, usually some form of soup made from a meagre amount of vegetables or from rotten meat. Tsvetan ate it nevertheless.

In an attempt to survive Tsvetan bore everything that he was subjected to until one day something happened that he could not ignore. A young woman who had been at the camp for several months had been reduced almost to a skeleton through excessive work and starvation. Try as she may she found it virtually impossible to eat the food that was provided and if she did sometimes manage to get the food down her it inevitably made her vomit for which she usually received a beating on top of having to clear up her own mess.

On this particular day one of the guards noticed her eating scraps from the plates that she was clearing away after the wardens' had eaten.

"Come here, you bitch," he yelled and as she stood before him he threw the leftover food onto the filthy floor and dragged her to it by the hair.

She sobbed from the pain and humiliation. Tsvetan was boiling over with rage but thought he could endure it. However, he was appalled to see that despite the humiliation she was suffering the desperate girl tried to eat what was on the ground and received a kick to the stomach for good measure. Tsvetan's control finally gave way and he jumped between them as the guard shaped to strike her again.

"I will not allow you to touch her again. You will kill her." The other inmates looked on in astonishment, fearing for Tsvetan and the girl.

"Move aside!" the guard demanded, but Tsvetan stood his ground.

"Touch the girl again and I know that God the almighty will show you no mercy." Tsvetan stood so firm and spoke with such confidence that the guard was disarmed and his courage failed him.

"Get the bitch out of here. I want her out of my sight," he barked out, but his authority had deserted him. Several inmates rushed forward and helped the pitiful girl to her feet and the guard stormed away. Tsvetan could see any faint hope he had of ever getting out of Belene Island receding into dust. He was sure he would face execution, but to his and everyone's surprise Tsvetan never suffered any repercussions from his actions.

Four days later the girl died and, as was the case with all of those that did not survive the brutality of the regime, she was buried in a shallow grave within the camp. Occasionally bad weather or foraging wild animals would bring their rotting corpses to the surface.

Despite everything Tsvetan and some of his fellow inmates tried to maintain a routine of prayer and worship. Although some prisoners were glad to be able to attend a makeshift mass held in the cell block in the evenings, most had no interest, believing that God had cast them aside. Others though, like Tsvetan, used their faith to help them get through the daily ordeals. Tsvetan's faith never wavered and he convinced himself that somehow, some day God would provide an answer. He clung firmly to this belief, because it meant that it was always worth it to try and carry on. He thought often of Tatyana. Having no news of her was the hardest thing of all. Against all the odds he maintained the unshakeable belief that somehow their paths would cross again.

Chapter Twenty Three

"Viktorov!" the guard shouted along the landing. "Get yourself over here!"

Tsvetan looked up wondering what he had done now. No doubt he was in contravention of some camp rule of which he had no prior knowledge. More senseless punishment, he assumed, but he knew he could handle it just as he had many times before. He mouthed a silent prayer and approached the guard.

"Put that damned broom down! You have an important visitor from the Party. Do you think she is interested in your filthy broom?" Tsvetan ignored the bad language, placed the broom against a wall as he passed and continued until he stood before the guard.

"You stink!" the guard announced. "I hope for your sake the commander does not object to your smell. Follow me!" he ordered. Tsvetan followed him trying to create some curiosity as to who was asking for him, but found that he was beyond curiosity.

They came to a halt outside the Governor's office The guard knocked politely, but to Tsvetan's surprise it was not the Governor's voice that replied but the voice of a woman.

"Come!" she ordered and the guard, now meek and respectful, opened the door.

"I have Viktorov here ma'am."

"*Father* Viktorov," she corrected him. "Send him in and leave us," she said.

"Yes, ma'am." The guard withdrew slowly, still respectfully facing the woman until he was out of the door and gone.

"Sit down, Father," she said politely pointing to a chair across the desk from her. Tsvetan did not need a second invitation. He had not sat on a soft chair for several years.

"You don't know me, Father," she began, but Tsvetan interjected at once.

"I do not know you," he confirmed, "But I know who you are. You are Vesela Nikolova, wife of Slavko Nikolov."

The woman, who was at least seventy years old maybe older, looked surprised. "How do you know this?" she demanded slightly irritated.

"God gives us the power of free and independent thought," Tsvetan replied. "Some of us choose to use it."

Vesela did not like this response. She tried to tell herself it was his impertinence that she objected to, but it was not that. His answer irritated her because it struck home. Had she become just part of the machine, a party drone? Had she lost her ability for independent thought? Tsvetan could see that for a moment he had gained the upper hand, but he did not play their games.

"You have nothing to fear from me," he said. "You are a powerful leader within the ruling party. I am a weak and humble priest in your custody. Just say what you want from me."

Vesela hesitated. This was not how she had planned it. She could see already that her offer would be spurned.

"You were a good friend to my husband. He mentions you all the time in his diaries," she told him.

Tsvetan sat motionless in the well upholstered chair meant for more important people than him. He did not like the fact that she had been reading Slavko Nikolov's private records. She was his wife, but had long since surrendered any rights attached to that position.

"I did not know he kept a diary," he replied.

"After the Party came to power I returned to Svishtov, to my old house. The diaries were by his bedside. I imagine he wrote his thoughts from the day last thing before going to sleep."

Tsvetan met her eyes with a look that seemed to judge her. "If you have read his diaries then you will know you broke his heart," he said. His eyes remained fixed on hers and she suffered under his hard gaze.

Her response was hopelessly predictable. "I had to go. The Party needed me and I was unable to operate openly. I saw the Party as the vehicle for improving people's lives. I still do. I did what was necessary."

As if to spare her he released her face from his scrutiny and looked away. He shared the same guilt as her.

"What is the point of acting to bring about good in the world if by doing so you break the hearts of those that love you? I know this to be wrong because I also carry this sin."

From reading her husband's diaries she had realised that Tsvetan was no ordinary man, but she had not expected him to be so quietly formidable. Her guilt over her treatment of Slavko was ever present. It did not take much to bring it to the surface. She now wanted to bring this encounter to an end. She would get straight to the point of her visit.

"I came here to make an offer to you that would allow you your freedom." She looked at him, hoping for some kind of response, but none was forthcoming. "You have only to renounce the Catholic Church and you will be released this very day. You do not even have to renounce God. You can walk free today, Father."

He stared hard at her. He had respected, even loved her husband, but he felt no respect for this woman.

"To renounce the Church I love is to renounce God. There is no freedom in renouncing what you believe in. I will remain here."

Vesela had expected it. Life was not everything to such a man. She had no power to hurt him; nothing she could take from him or give to him that would make a difference. She felt small and uncomfortable in his presence. Vesela Nikolova stood up and tried to regain her previous authority. She walked to the door, opened it wide and called for the guard. Tsvetan got up from his chair and replaced it neatly in front of the Governor's desk. Quietly he walked from the room without acknowledging her.

*

Over a period of six months there had been a particularly large increase in the number of inmates as a result of which the work schedules of the existing prisoners became impossible and they regularly failed to accomplish their allotted daily work. The wardens only responded to this with beatings and food deprivation which in turn made it harder to reach the targets they were set.

As a result of the expansion of the camp population new wardens were recruited from the local towns and villages. Amongst them was Dido, a good natured young man with whom Tsvetan had grown up. The first time that they saw each other Tsvetan recognised Dido instantly. However, it seemed that Dido had not recognised him. Tsvetan was unsure whether this was genuinely the case – after all his appearance had changed a great deal since being at the camp – or if Dido was reluctant, even frightened to acknowledge him.

The citizens of Belene and Svishtov, the towns closest to the island, had been oblivious to what was happening at the camp. The overwhelming majority of the local people believed the official explanation that the inmates at the camp were dangerous enemies of the state. The new recruits to Belene Island therefore had no clue as to what they were letting themselves in for. Some adapted quickly and became just as harsh in their treatment of inmates as their cynical comrades. A few, however, were appalled at what they encountered and found it, emotionally at least, almost as difficult as the inmates to get through the day.

One of those that found it particularly hard was Dido and this was compounded by the realisation that his erstwhile friend, Tsvetan was amongst the prisoners. He remembered Tsvetan as a serious, but kind-hearted soul and could not swallow the idea of him being an enemy of the state. Anyway, Dido found the cruelty at Belene Island unacceptable even if the prisoners *were* guilty of some crime. One day, he could stand it no longer and knew if he did not do something to help Tsvetan he would never be able to live with himself or hold his head up in his own town.

"Tsvetan, it is me, Dido," he whispered to him on the first occasion that he had a chance to speak to him relatively safely.

"I know it is you. I thought you had not recognised me," replied Tsvetan cautiously.

Dido looked around him terrified that they may be overheard. "I want to help you," he said.

"It helps me to know that you are around Dido and that you acknowledge our shared history. It means a great deal."

Dido was a simpler soul than Tsvetan and was unable to see how that could make a difference. "No, that is no help to you. I can only help you if I find a way to get you out of here."

Just at that moment another inmate appeared. Tsvetan and Dido had both learned that on Belene Island it was best to trust no one, not even another prisoner. Dido walked over to the prisoner and barked out an order. Tsvetan went on his way.

In the years he had been in Belene Island camp it had never occurred to Tsvetan to try and escape. He had always tried to keep his head down, do as he was told whenever possible and trust in God. This was his way of surviving. Now the idea was in his head he could not rid himself of it. He did not fear failure or worry about what would happen to him if he were caught. If this happened and he was executed then so be it. He would bear it. But what of Dido? He knew that Dido had a wife and three children, as well as parents that relied on him. He did not need to risk everything. Only Tsvetan had nothing to lose.

At the first chance he had Tsvetan put this to Dido telling him that he would not allow him to risk his own life or the lives of those that depended on him. Dido, nevertheless remained firm.

"If I don't help you I will never be able to look them in the eye again. If I do nothing what sort of man am I? My mind is made up. You are getting out of here." Before Tsvetan could answer Dido turned on his heel and walked away.

Chapter Twenty Four

Tsvetan's incarceration at the Belene Island Labour Camp was a predicament beyond anything Milen could help with. Milen was a well-respected member of the Party with considerable influence. He was also a senior officer in the notorious State Security Forces, an organisation feared by Party members almost as much as by those outside of it. However, he had no influence over the fate of the inmates of Belene Island.

He had become aware that Comrade Vesela Nikolova was planning to speak to Tsvetan, perhaps she already had. Given Tsvetan's close friendship with her deceased husband, Comrade Vesela felt an obligation to the young priest and would be inclined to treat him with leniency if at all possible. However, Milen also guessed what approach she would take with Tsvetan and he knew that Tsvetan would not consider making any sort of deal with her. He better than anybody knew his friend's stubbornness. He had been witness to it many times over the years.

He was stumped and felt immense guilt that he was letting Tsvetan down, but what could he do? Then suddenly out of the blue he had a visit from Dido. Milen had not seen his childhood friend for a number of years. He had heard that he had become a warden at Belene Island which had surprised him. Knowing Dido as he did he was sure he was finding it tough.

Dido had been unsure about approaching Milen. They were old friends of course, but almost everything in Bulgaria had been turned on its head in the last few years and Milen was now in a powerful position within the Communist Party. He would never have trusted him to put friendship above Party, but Tsvetan had been adamant.

"Talk to Milen." he had urged. "I trust him more than I trust myself. Talk to him."

Dido remembered how it had been between Milen and Tsvetan as children. For years they were inseparable, like two peas in the same pod, but would that still count? Despite Tsvetan's assurances he approached the matter carefully.

"I came to see you," Dido said once the formalities of greeting were over, "Because I thought you might like to hear word of Tsvetan. I remember how close you were."

Immediately Milen's mask dropped and he pressed Dido to tell him everything he knew about Tsvetan's situation. "Have you spoken with him? Is he holding up? Please tell me he is alright."

Dido was somewhat taken aback. Milen showed all the concern that one would expect from a close friend, but what went on at Belene Island Camp was done in the name of the Party to which he was committed. Dido wondered how he lived with his own conscience.

Cautiously Dido gave Milen the news about his friend that he seemed to crave, but still he lacked the courage, or the trust to confide his plan to him. Then all of a sudden Milen himself seized upon the possibility of getting his friend out of the wretched camp.

"Dido, we could get him out. If we work together we could free him. Much would fall to you on the inside, but I would be ready to do whatever would be required. We could do it, Dido. We could do it if you are game."

Dido could not resist a wry smile. Milen must be genuine. Although he was considerably more powerful than Dido, a basic grade prison warden, he was still taking risks speaking in this way. Why would he do that if his motives were not sound? It appeared that the faith that Tsvetan had in Milen was justified. He made a decision from which there was no going back.

"I am game as you put it, Milen," he said. "I will do whatever I must to free him. That is the reason I am here."

*

Life for Tatyana had become pointless without Tsvetan as her compass. She had returned to live at home where she came under constant pressure from her mother to forget about Tsvetan and start building a new life for herself.

"You are still young, Tanya, and also beautiful. You have your whole life ahead of you. You cannot throw it all away for the sake of a man you will never see again. You need to get yourself out there, find a young man perhaps."

Usually Tatyana reacted angrily when her mother spoke to her in this way, but on this occasion she just lacked the energy. She knew her mother meant well, but the truth was that her mother had never understood her daughter's love for the priest.

"If he loves you, as you insist he does, then surely he has betrayed you by taking the vows of the Catholic Church," Yordana continued.

This was Tatyana's weak point. Tsvetan had often told her that, had he not lost her in those early days when they were unaware of each other's love, things would have worked out differently. However, when she thought back to the crucial moments in their short history she felt only disappointment in Tsvetan's actions or lack of them. When she told him that she was moving to Plovdiv why did he not speak up? When coincidently he found himself in Plovdiv why did it take him a month before he even sought her out? When fate intervened and he discovered she had moved suddenly to Sofia, why did he not search for her? It would have been easy to go to her grandmother in Plovdiv to ask for an address, but he did nothing. She was sure that Tsvetan did love her, but was his love for the Catholic Church always stronger even then?

"He has not betrayed me," she replied at last to her mother. "He has not betrayed me and I will not betray him."

Her mother's response was not sympathetic. "I did not betray your father by marrying Cleto because he was gone from me. The same would apply to you. Face it Tanya, your priest, he is lost."

Tatyana ran from the room. Not on this occasion because of anger towards her mother, although Yordana interpreted her action in that way, but because she knew her defences had been breached. She needed to be alone to work things out without her mother continually pressing her for some sort of answer.

Nevertheless, her mother did continue to press her. The pressure from Yordana urging her daughter to re-enter normal society was persuasive and unrelenting. Feeling the strain Tatyana sought Cleto's advice as she knew that he understood her feelings towards Tsvetan and that he also liked and respected the young priest.

"I know you love him, Bella Mia, but how long can you live in this limbo, this purgatory?" He could see that she was close to tears and he knew it was because he had accurately described her situation. "Carrying on as you are is not possible, not forever anyway. You have many more years on this Earth. You cannot spend all your life as a widow to a man that was never truly yours." Tatyana felt overwhelmed with sadness. As her stepfather spoke she could feel Tsvetan slowly slipping from her grasp.

*

There comes a time, a moment in most people's lives when they know there is something they must do. Such a moment had arrived for Dido. He would get his friend out of the filthy camp at Belene Island or die trying. He did not share his plan with his wife with whom he had previously shared everything because he knew she would do all in her power to stop him and this could only lead to anguish for both of them. Also if things went wrong he did not want her to carry the burden of knowing and being regarded as an accessory.

Slowly in his own mind Dido formed a plan. He now knew the routine at Belene Island and he could see the times at which the security arrangements were at their weakest. In truth the security within the camp relied as much on the passivity of the inmates as it did on the vigilance of the guards. There were times when less guards were on duty and those that were supposed to be watching over the inmates were less diligent, relying to a large extent on the belief that the inmates were too worn down to attempt anything.

In the summer when the weather was fine there was a tendency to lock the prisoners into their compounds earlier than was prescribed so the guards could enjoy the late evening sunshine. This enjoyment usually involved a bottle of rakia that the guards would pass around until it was empty. This would be the time to put Tsvetan's planned escape into action. Dido's part in the plan would be to free Tsvetan from the compound and get him through or over the perimeter fence. It would then be down to Tsvetan to get himself to the shore where Milen would pick him up in the family's old fishing boat.

Dido concluded that the plan was simple, but sound. Getting Tsvetan out of the building that held him would not be difficult. The wardens each had keys to all the buildings in the camp and although the wardens were supposed to operate in twos at all times nobody conformed to this rule, particularly not when the inmates were safely locked in for the night. The difficulty would be in helping Tsvetan get beyond the camp's perimeter fence. Finally after examining the perimeter as best he could without arousing suspicion, Dido decided he would have to cut a hole in the fence beforehand and try and disguise the opening in the period leading up to the planned escape. He selected a point in the fencing where he could make the cut without being seen. Now all that was left was to agree a date with Milen.

*

Since the day when Cleto's neighbour had allowed him to use his phone the two men had become good friends. The doctor enjoyed a drink in the evening and often invited Cleto to join him. He was fascinated with Cleto's extensive knowledge of wine and always tried to get hold of something a bit different, usually from the black market, whenever his friend was expected. They were sitting having a glass of Italian Chianti for which the doctor had paid a small fortune when Cleto started to tell him his worries concerning Tatyana.

"I think I have persuaded her to try and forget about Father Viktorov, but she still just sits at home with a book in her hand, not even reading it half the time. Her mother and I are beside ourselves with worry."

The doctor's eyes lit up in a way that surprised Cleto given what he had just told him, but soon the reason for this became clear.

"She is a beautiful girl," said the doctor, "At least so my son thinks." He looked at his neighbour mischievously. "As you know he recently returned home to take up a post at the new Pirogov Hospital here in Sofia. He does not seem to be thinking much about the job.

The only thing he has noticed since his return is your lovely daughter."

Cleto looked at him with interest. He had met the son briefly outside the house and thought him a very pleasant and polite young man. Although he regarded Bulgarian men as somewhat rough in their features when compared to his own countrymen, he could see that the young doctor could be regarded as reasonably handsome.

"Bring him round for dinner," Cleto urged him, "And bring your dear wife too. It is about time I repaid you for drinking all your expensive wine. Who knows, they might really get along." The deal was struck and the two men toasted their attempts at matchmaking with another glass of the rare Chianti.

Yordana received the news of the dinner invitation with excitement, but also with trepidation. "It is an excellent idea, Cleto, but what can I give them to eat. They seem to have access to the black market, but I have to rely on rations. It is fine as long as you realise you can have very little to eat between now and then. Everything must be saved for that evening."

Cleto groaned in a good humoured manner. Depriving him of food even in such a good cause was a serious matter.

Tatyana's response was one of indifference. She had no idea who the boy was and was not especially interested in finding out, but a dinner invitation was a rare thing and she assured her stepfather that she would look forward to it.

Although Tatyana did not start the evening with any intentions regarding the young doctor his charm offensive towards her was almost irresistible. Soon she found herself laughing at his jokes and listening with interest to his many stories about life in Varna where he had studied medicine. The city on the Black Sea sounded enchanting and his life there, swimming every day and frequenting seaside bars and cafes in the evenings seemed idyllic.

"I am surprised you passed your doctors' exams with all the fun you were having," she chided.

Stanimir laughed. "No, I took that seriously enough," he assured her. He looked affectionately towards his father. "The old man would never have forgiven me," he said, apparently still looking at his father, but keeping a close eye on Tatyana's reactions. He need not have worried. He still had her full attention.

After the doctor and his family left, Yordana was keen to get an opinion of the boy from her daughter, but as usual Cleto came to her rescue.

"Let the poor girl be!" he told her. "Is she not allowed any thoughts or opinions without sharing them with you?"

"It is alright, Cleto," said Tatyana wanting to retain the pleasant mood of the evening. "Mama naturally wants to know if I am in love with him."

Yordana smiled at Tatyana, glad to be able to have a fun conversation with her daughter for once. "Well that would be asking a lot," Yordana admitted. "Did you at least find him attractive?"

Tatyana continued to indulge her mother. "Cute, I would call him rather than attractive. He is too much of a boy to be called attractive," she said smiling wickedly at her mother.

"Well, it's a start!" her mother exclaimed with relief.

"No mother, it is not a start or even a finish. It was just a nice evening with some good company. They are a lovely family."

For the first time in a while Cleto felt happy and at peace. It was not important to him whether anything transpired between the young Stanimir and his beautiful stepdaughter. It was just perfect for him to sit amongst a smiling family again with their playful banter bouncing between them.

Lying in bed that evening Tatyana reflected more on the stories of Stanimir's life in Varna than on the boy himself. What stuck with her was the carefree nature of Stanimir's life in the city by the sea. One might have expected that living and studying in the fashionable city of Perugia would throw up similar opportunities and indeed it had. However, even before he came back into her life with a chance meeting in Florence, her hopeless love for Tsvetan had been weighing her down, taking the edge off her happiness.

Chapter Twenty Five

It was unusual for Milen to contact Tatyana. She had not seen him since the day he helped them re-enter Bulgaria. The message had said that he was in Sofia for twenty four hours and they should meet. Against all the odds she hoped he may have some news about Tsvetan.

It had become so unusual for Tatyana to put some nice clothes on and go into the city her mother wanted to know exactly where she was off to and with whom. Tatyana knew that her mother's hope was that she would be going to meet Stanimir and she cleverly used this to get her mother off the scent.

"That is my little secret," she said with a wicked smile. Her mother looked at her as if they were two conspirators. As she left the house Tatyana knew that she would probably come to regret this unspoken lie, but for now she was just glad to get away without some lengthy explanation.

Milen had suggested they meet on Maria Luiza Boulevard by the Lions' Bridge. As she approached she could see him leaning against the railings, looking as usual as if he did not have a care in the world. However, she was aware that if he had asked to meet her then he had something very specific on his mind. They greeted each other with an affectionate kiss. Tatyana would never forget what she already owed this man. As is his way, Milen came straight to the point.

Tatyana could hardly take in what she had just been told. She remembered Dido from her youth in Svishtov. He had been a pleasant shy young man, quite unremarkable she would have judged. How wrong could she be? Tatyana was elated at the news although she immediately realised how dangerous it would be. Within a very short time elation gave way to anxiety.

"But if you do get him out they will soon find him again. He is well known now. It would only be a matter of time until the authorities got to know his whereabouts."

Milen was quiet for a moment. He was not so sure about this next part of the plan.

"I know it sounds crazy, but he is planning to escape through Romania," he admitted finally.

Tatyana's first reaction was to think it was indeed crazy, but wherever he went it would be difficult to get from there to safety. For Tsvetan Romania was probably marginally safer than Bulgaria. At least nobody would be actively looking for him there. Milen could read the doubt in her beautiful face. It occurred to him that it must be years since he had seen her smile.

"It should also help his escape," he told her. "Once the wardens realise he is gone they will be anticipating him heading for the Bulgarian mainland. It should give him extra time."

Tatyana looked at Milen with interest and admiration. He was a successful and apparently committed member of the Communist Party with considerable power and influence, yet he would put all of this at risk to help his friend. She was of course aware that he had done this before, but this time the odds against him pulling it off without consequences for himself seemed very slim indeed. It was clear to Tatyana that for Milen this was the last thing to be considered. He must love Tsvetan as much as she did she thought, perhaps more.

"If he is not coming to Bulgaria then I must go with him," she said taking Milen completely by surprise. He had come to tell her of the plan because he knew that Tsvetan would want her to know. He had not expected this.

"That is impossible." Milen was adamant that she could not be involved, but Tatyana was not taking no for an answer.

"I will go in the boat with you. I am not some useless city girl. It will be better if there are two of us."

Milen tried to object, but it was obvious he was wasting his breath. "But we are committed to doing this on Thursday evening, in just two days. How could you be ready? I will not delay it. It will just add to the danger."

"I will be ready," she told him, "Have no fear of that."

On Thursday morning Tatyana appeared in her mother's room just after breakfast. Cleto had left early to go to the factory. The boys were in school. Tatyana and her mother were alone in the house. Yordana could see that her daughter was dressed for a journey.

"What is it, Tanya? Where are you going?" She could sense that Tatyana had something monumental to impart. It frightened her.

"I am catching a train to Svishtov in an hour's time," she told her. "I cannot be sure, but unless things change in the world I may not be back."

Her mother stared at her. "What are you doing child? It is that damned priest isn't it? What on earth are you planning?"

Tatyana slowly told her mother almost the whole story only leaving out the fact that she intended to be in the boat. She related it as sensitively as possible, aware that Yordana had no time to take it all in. In ten minutes she would be gone, probably for ever.

"You can't do it, Tanya. I won't allow it. I won't let you throw your life away. You might be killed."

Tatyana took the hand of her totally distraught mother who was sobbing uncontrollably.

"Mama, I am going. I am not throwing my life away. This is my only chance of life. You must try and understand. I love him. I have always and will always love him."

Yordana grasped at straws. "What about poor Cleto? He knows nothing. He will come home and find his darling girl gone. You can't do this to him."

At this Tatyana's courage almost failed her and the tears flowed. "Mama, tell him...tell him I love him like a father."

Slowly she got to her feet releasing her mother's hand like that of a child who she had just led across the road. She bent down and kissed the top of Yordana's head and without another word between them left the house. Yordana did not move.

Tatyana had almost no luggage, aware that once on her way through Romania it would only slow them down. In her one small bag she had her meagre savings, a change of underclothes, a small toy from her childhood and her stepfather's loaded revolver.

Chapter Twenty Six

The day arrived all too quickly for Dido. He was not ready, but he knew further delay would not help. He would probably never be ready. The simple fact was he was terrified. Yesterday he had gone to an area of the perimeter fence that he had previously identified as the escape point. It was where the fence came quite close to the camp buildings forming a fairly narrow alleyway between the perimeter and the prisoners' compounds. The alleyway did not go anywhere and, other than to take a leak, nobody ever used this area. He easily cut a hole in the wire and placed it back together. It would not be noticed.

Dido got ready for work as normal and said goodbye to the children as cheerfully as he could manage. He then gave his wife such a loving kiss that she thought he had something else in mind.

"Go on!" she said, "You'll be late for work."

Reluctantly Dido dragged himself from the house and set off down the road like a man taking himself to the gallows. Before he crossed the floating bridge to the island he looked back at the town where he had spent his whole life. Everything and everybody that he loved was there. As he turned to cross the bridge he wondered if he would ever see the little town again.

*

When Tatyana reached the shore she could see Milen already at the boat, preparing the vessel as if for a fishing trip. He heard footsteps and looked up to see Tatyana walking nervously towards him. Suddenly he was reminded of occasions years ago when she would shyly approach the boat in the hope of getting a few minutes together with Tsvetan. She would ask pointless and inane questions about fishing, a subject in which she had no interest. It brought a smile to Milen's face now as he thought about it. Often he would ask her if she wanted to accompany them, but she always declined. She lived in hope that Tsvetan would ask her, but he never did. Even then Milen used to tell him what a fool he was. If only he had listened.

Tatyana had endured a stressful train journey that had taken seven hours instead of the scheduled four, with a three hour wait at Levski. At one point she was terrified that Milen might have left without her.

"You've cut it fine," he commented as if they were about to go on an organised sightseeing trip along the Danube. Tatyana smiled. She was glad to be able to continue as if it were a normal day for as long as possible.

"I thought the Communist Party were going to make the trains run on time?" she quipped.

"Patience, comrade," replied Milen. "It is central to next year's plan." They both laughed and then suddenly stopped as if they had simultaneously remembered what was in front of them.

"We might as well get going," suggested Milen, focussing albeit reluctantly on the business in hand. "It is best if people see us fishing at the normal sites. We may need some sort of alibi." and then added, "Well I might anyway. You will be in Romania on your way to somewhere more romantic than this." Tatyana smiled at his confidence that the whole enterprise would inevitably end successfully.

"That is the crazy thing," Tatyana replied. "If you block out the horrific things that are perpetrated on that beautiful island, you would say there are few more romantic spots on this earth. I used to think so anyway."

Milen did not answer her directly. What Tatyana said was true, but Milen did not want to think such thoughts just at this moment. Nostalgia is not going to help us now, he thought to himself.

"Come on, get in. We have work to do," he said and within minutes they were in the middle of the river to all intents and purposes focussed on catching fish.

*

Dido sat with the other guards in the late evening sunshine taking his turn with the rakia bottle without actually drinking anything. He needed to remain sharp. After half an hour he got up and went to wander off.

"Where are you going, comrade?" one of the wardens asked him jovially.

"Well someone has to make sure the women prisoners are alright," he replied with a wink.

"Well don't let her make too much noise," the warden replied. "We're trying to relax here." The others laughed.

"You'll be lucky to find one who doesn't stink like a bear," one of the younger men warned him. "I would rather wait until I get home," he added.

A fat brute of a man who seemed already to be well under the influence of the rakia scoffed at this suggestion.

"It's alright for you, brother. We've seen your missus. Anyone would be happy to wait for that."

By this time Dido had made his way to the compounds. The lewd conversation that he had started continued in his absence and nobody took the least bit of notice of what he was doing. He unlocked the door of the cell block that housed Tsvetan and looked around. Tsvetan saw him immediately and within seconds the door was locked again and Dido was leading him to the hole in the fence. The other inmates showed no interest in his sudden absence. Being collected at night only meant one thing and those that had seen him leave were simply glad it was not them.

With no ceremony of any kind Tsvetan climbed through the hole in the wire that his friend had cut and disappeared. Dido had just re-joined the group of wardens as the leader of the evening shift came running over barking out orders as he came.

"We've just had word of a planned escape. It's one of the Catholic bastards, the priest, Viktorov. Bring him here!"

It did not take long to establish that Tsvetan was missing. Two groups of wardens were quickly assembled. The first group included Dido. He was surprised and frightened when the two groups were told to go through the forest towards the Romanian side of the island. Even worse, two other guards were sent by jeep to go directly to the river bank. Someone had betrayed them, but who and how much did they know? His first thought was that it could be Milen, but he dismissed that, annoyed at himself that he could even think it.

In fact it was Milen, waiting on the shore who was now most at risk. Dido felt helpless, but there was nothing he could do, not now anyway. He thought of his wife and children waiting for him at home. Would their wait be in vain? He pushed the thought aside. He was up to his neck in it now. All he could do was try and see it through.

Chapter Twenty Seven

Tsvetan's heart was pumping. His feet were in tatters and bleeding badly. His head ached.

"Keep going; just keep going!" he told himself again and again, but his body was getting to the point where it could no longer obey his commands. He could hear them behind him, not far now. If he did not reach the shore in the next few minutes they would be on him. He just hoped to God that Milen would be there. He had promised. When had he ever promised and failed to deliver? Never! He would surely not let him down now.

The prison wardens from the Belene Labour Camp had only limited experience of pursuing prisoners across this part of the island. Since the camp opened in 1949 only four inmates had breached the perimeter of the labour camp and none of those had made it this far.

Tsvetan had expected to surprise everyone. He was a model prisoner who appeared to accept the punishments and hardships handed down to him without complaint. Surely no one had for a moment expected him to try to escape. He had anticipated gaining some advantage from the element of surprise. He had also thought to further confound the guards by heading not for the shores of Bulgaria's mainland but towards Romania. The prison population was exclusively Bulgarian and most inmates would have regarded flight to Romania as more dangerous than staying put. Tsvetan had anticipated that by the time the guards had organised their pursuit of him he would already be half way to the shore. However, to his dismay they seemed to know his intended route and were now no more than a few hundred metres behind him.

Tsvetan could see the light ahead of him indicating that he was on the edge of the forest. With a renewed energy he thrust forward and burst out of the forest onto the gravelly shore, squinting against the sudden onslaught of light. The small pebbles were hard beneath his bare feet, but he hardly noticed the pain. He looked up and with relief saw Milen's thirty year old boat.

Despite the situation his mind was suddenly filled with memories of himself and Milen as young men fishing on the banks of the Danube in this very boat. It was a wonderful memory of life before communist occupation; a memory of another time. Tsvetan's eyes scanned the shoreline desperately, searching for his friend. Then he saw him. Fifty metres from the boat Milen's apparently lifeless body lay on the ground while the tide lapped around him. With the guards almost upon him Tsvetan was faced with an agonising decision: should he run to Milen to see if there was any life left in him or to the possible safety of the boat?

There was only one choice. As he got to him he realised that his dear friend was still breathing, although barely conscious. He was bleeding from the chest and the spilled blood was mingling with the water that now surrounded him creating a lurid pink colour. Tsvetan looked around now desperate to get Milen to the boat. As he looked towards the edge of the forest he saw the bodies of two wardens. He turned back to Milen just as his friend briefly became conscious.

"They were here waiting for us. I had not seen them. The next thing I knew one of them had fired and I fell."

Tsvetan was racked with remorse. Milen had done this for him. Why had he allowed it? Now his greatest friend in all the world was lying here bleeding to death so that he might live. Vainly, he tried to pull him to safety.

"No, Tsvetan, leave me. It is too late." His voice was fading, but holding his friend's arm he continued. "We were betrayed. They were waiting for us. I killed the one that shot me from where I lay. The other approached me, but he did not realise someone else was in the boat. As he raised his gun to finish me off Tatyana shot him through the head."

Tsvetan's pulse was racing. He could not believe what he had just heard. "Tatyana? She is here?"

"She is in the boat. I told her to stay down," Milen spluttered as blood trickled from his mouth. Any minute now the guards would be on the shore. Tsvetan could hear their boots on the narrow forest path.

"Quick, get to the boat. She is waiting for you." As Tsvetan hesitated Milen managed to raise his voice. "Go! Please go otherwise it was all for nothing."

Tsvetan got to his feet not knowing if he still wanted to survive, but there was Tatyana. He could not lose her too. He turned to go, but had one last question for his dying friend.

"Who was it, Milen? Who betrayed us?"

With his last breath Milen was still concerned for his friends. "Don't tell her Tsvetan. It will destroy her."

Tsvetan did not know what his friend was saying. He tried to scrutinise Milen's face for an answer, but saw only pain.

"I don't understand, Milen. What should I not tell her?"

Milen looked at Tsvetan for the last time. "Don't tell Tatyana it was her mother that betrayed you."

Somehow Tsvetan dragged himself towards the boat weighed down by the knowledge his friend had imparted to him as he died. Suddenly five guards emerged from the forest blinking as the sunlight temporarily blinded them. Tsvetan ran to the boat in which Tatyana lay in terror. He started to push it out into the river, but it was hopeless. He would never get away before the guards reached the water's edge. The guards approached, shooting as they did so, but one of them hung back. He lifted his gun carefully and shot three of his colleagues with just three shots. Two died instantly, the third looked up at Dido with incomprehension in his face, then slumped to the ground.

The final guard could not think clearly or quickly enough. He just looked at Dido for some sort of explanation. Suddenly his brain kicked into gear and he raised his gun. Tsvetan desperately heaved at the boat. From within Tatyana looked out at the scene of carnage. Her whole body was shaking as her first shot flew past the guard ricocheting off the trees. The guard turned to face her with terror in his eyes. Her second shot was true and he fell to his knees and slowly toppled over onto his face.

Dido tore across the gravelly sand just as Tsvetan got the small vessel afloat in the water. Dido was about to clamber into the boat, but Tsvetan stopped him.

"You are not thinking clearly, Dido. If you come with us you will never see your family again. You must stay here. You can tell the camp commandant your own story. None of these wardens can contradict you."

Dido hesitated. He knew Tsvetan was right, but his courage was failing him. What if no one believed his account? What if the person who had betrayed them knew of his role in the attempted escape? Tsvetan saw the fear in his eyes.

"It is for the best my friend. You must be strong. God will protect you."

Dido nodded agreement. He would stay and take his chances. Tsvetan hugged him and then taking the revolver from Tatyana shot his friend in the arm. He fell to the ground clutching his arm where the bullet had entered. Bewilderment spread across his face, then all of a sudden he understood. Tsvetan and Tatyana grabbed the oars and rowed for their lives. Minutes later the second wave of guards appeared on the shore, but they were too late. The small boat was almost out of sight heading for the Romanian coast.

In the boat Tatyana was still shaking. Panic and fear were etched on her face. They were now quite close to the Romanian shore and some decisions needed to be made. Although neither of them were clear what to do next, no words passed between them. The horror they had experienced was too raw to talk about. Also they each had added burdens that rendered them silent. Tatyana could not believe she had ended the lives of two men and left them lying there on the sand. Others would think she was a hero, but she felt only revulsion. What had happened to her country? What was happening to its young people? A country that had survived a major war was now at war with itself.

Tsvetan was consumed with grief for his friend, still racked with guilt that he had allowed him to take such risks on his behalf. He thought of their friendship over the years and it occurred to him, not for the first time, that it had usually been Milen that had made the sacrifices. It had been Milen that had given out sound advice and he who again and again had failed to listen. He asked himself whether he would have made the ultimate sacrifice that his friend had now made so that he could live. He hoped that had he been tested he would have proved himself worthy of that special friendship that existed between them. He could not be sure.

His thoughts then passed to the one that had betrayed them, surely the person who was most responsible for the corpses lying on the shore of Belene Island. His mind went back to Yordana's sudden and unexpected release. At the time he felt only joy that Tatyana had been spared the pain of losing her mother, but now he had experienced Belene Island for himself he began to wonder. Once sentenced there was no way back unless a deal could be struck. Yordana had told her daughter that she had been released because the authorities knew she was innocent of the charges. Tsvetan knew quite well that none of the inmates at the camp were guilty of the ludicrous charges against them. As far as the authorities were concerned this would never constitute a reason to release them.

He remembered his meeting with Vesela Nikolova and wondered whether she had interviewed Tatyana's mother and if so what she had asked of her in exchange for her release. Had the woman never considered that she might be condemning her own daughter to death?

Milen's dying wish had been that he should not tell Tatyana of her mother's betrayal. "Don't tell her Tsvetan. It will destroy her." he had warned. Nevertheless, Tsvetan's instinct was to tell Tatyana because he believed they should not have a secret of this magnitude between them. He thought long and hard and as he did so the terrible picture of Milen lying bleeding on the ground returned to haunt him. Maybe it would forever.

Surely his belief that he should tell Tatyana the truth was just typical of the self-indulgence that he had been guilty of all his life? How often had he regretted not listening to the wisdom of his friend? Milen was right. It would destroy Tatyana and in turn destroy them. Their future, if they even had one, was uncertain. It was highly likely that Tatyana would never see her family again. Surely she should be allowed her memories. For once he would follow Milen's advice.

Chapter Twenty Eight

Tsvetan turned to speak to Tatyana, but saw at once that she was fast asleep, no doubt completely exhausted. Reluctant to dock the boat on the Romanian side of the Danube without some sort of plan, they had simply drifted along the middle of the river with no particular direction in mind. That they were a considerable distance from Belene Island had been enough to satisfy them so far. It was getting dark and the few figures they had seen on the Romanian mainland were now obscured from them. They had seemingly not attracted any attention up to now, but then why would they? Tsvetan felt certain that an old fishing boat drifting along on the huge river was as familiar a sight in Romania as it was at home in Bulgaria. The problems would arise as soon as they went ashore.

There was a large canteen of water on board and some bread and cheese that Milen had the forethought to stow on the boat before setting off. To Tsvetan's relief he had also brought clothes and shoes so he was at last able to dispose of the prison rags that had been his only clothing since arriving at the camp. They could manage for a while, but some proper plan of action was urgently needed. Tsvetan thought about the options open to them. None of them were particularly encouraging. Landing in Romania and presenting themselves to the authorities could not be considered. The two countries had similar Soviet sponsored Communist regimes and an enemy of the state in Bulgaria would be seen as an enemy of Romania. They would either be returned to Bulgaria or, more likely, executed on the spot.

If they stayed on the Danube heading west until they reached Yugoslavia they might have better prospects, although even this was doubtful. Besides it was approximately two hundred kilometres to the province of Serbia and Tsvetan was unsure whether the old boat was still capable of such a journey. Also they would have to go ashore from time to time either in Bulgaria or Romania with all the risks associated with that.

By the time Tatyana woke up Tsvetan had made up his mind. Landing in Romania was, he decided, not an option. Presenting themselves to the authorities was suicide and trying to get through Romania was pointless given it was completely surrounded by Communist states. Bulgaria too was surrounded on its northern and western borders with Communist regimes. To the east was the Black Sea. As far as Tsvetan could see they had no option but to land in Bulgaria and head south. They would have to try and get through and out of Bulgaria into Greece the only western aligned state in the region.

Tatyana woke up frozen. She had no interest in where they were nor where they were going. Tsvetan could see that she needed to eat, drink and get warm. With no thought for their future needs he watched her drink half of their water supply and eat most of their food. To get her warm he wrapped her in a tarpaulin and held her to him until at last she seemed to have recovered herself enough to discuss what they should do. She was initially shocked at Tsvetan's suggestion that they should try their luck back through Bulgaria into Greece, but as he outlined the various options she came to realise there was no real alternative.

"By my reckoning we must be somewhere near Nikopol by now," he told her. "In fact those lights across there must be the town. We should go ashore now and head into town first thing in the morning. From there it is about two hundred kilometres to Plovdiv. Have you any money?" he asked suddenly.

"Yes, I have all my savings with me. It is not a lot, but it will be enough," she replied. Tsvetan looked mightily relieved.

Just at that moment, with their plans now set, Tatyana noticed a searchlight scanning the river. Too frightened to speak she nudged him and silently pointed to the light that was fast approaching.

Tsvetan looked in horror. "The lights are from a boat. It must be border guards either from Bulgaria or Romania."

Their small boat was just beyond the range of the lights, but as the vessel got closer he could now just about make out voices drifting on the wind, Romanian voices. Not knowing what else to do he suddenly grabbed at the oars and starting rowing furiously in the direction of the Bulgarian mainland.

"Tsvetan, it is hopeless. We can never outrun them."

Tsvetan ignored her and carried on rowing although his body was aching and what strength he had left after the deprivation of the camp was starting to fail him. Just when it seemed impossible the lights moved to face the Romanian border indicating that the boat was turning back. At once he stopped rowing and slumped forward, holding his heaving chest as if to prevent it from detaching itself from the rest of his body. Tatyana watched in terrified silence as the lights from the patrol boat receded. Soon the lights of the boat were just a speck in the distance.

Slowly Tsvetan recovered his composure. "That seals it!" He exclaimed. "We must land in Bulgaria. We can stop in Plovdiv for a while until we can think of some way of getting into Greece. Mrs Marinova, my landlady from back then will take us in."

Tatyana looked at him long and hard. "I am scared Tsvetan," she said, voicing for the first time what he could plainly see for himself. "I'm not sure I can do it."

"We can make it together," he said trying desperately to reassure her when in fact he had no real faith in the plan himself.

"But are we together, Tsvetan?" she asked him. "Will we ever be truly together like other couples? Will we ever be lovers?" Here on this boat she had decided that she would make her stand. Depending on what he said she would either face whatever was thrown at them together even if it cost her life or she would put ashore in Nikopol and take her chances alone from there.

"I have never asked you, Tsvetan, to make a final choice between me and your church. I have always been afraid of the answer I would get. But I must ask you now. I love you and have done since I was little more than a child. You say you love me. You must withdraw your vows or it is over for us. It is your choice."

Tsvetan looked at her with his beautiful green eyes, the colour of the forest after it rains. It was one of the features that had first attracted her to him. Despite all his hardships at Belene Island they still shone stubbornly with hope. Inside she was falling apart.

What had she done? She had tried to push him to a place where he could not go and now surely she would pay for her folly. He raised his head proudly, his slim shoulders and straight back held him erect in spite of all the beatings he had taken. He took both her hands in his and for the first time she dared to hope.

"When Milen told me you were in the boat, that you had risked everything for me, it was then that I knew. Tatyana, amidst all that chaos and fear, I made the choice then."

She fell into his arms and he held her tightly, not as a friend, not even as a dear friend. He did not hold her as a priest comforts a parishioner. He held her as a man holds the woman he loves.

Chapter Twenty Nine

At just after midnight Tsvetan and Tatyana rowed to the bank of the River Danube on the Bulgarian side. There was very little moon and so as they stepped out of their boat and dragged it ashore it was difficult to see exactly where they were. The only lights they could see were a safe distance away in the town which Tsvetan felt sure was Nikopol.

"It is so hard to see. I can't make out where we have landed," said Tsvetan continuing to look around for something by which to get his bearings. Tatyana, deciding it was safe to do so, walked up the bank to give herself a better view of the area while Tsvetan looked on anxiously. She returned to Tsvetan and the boat before speaking.

"We seem to be on the edge of a field," she reported. "I can't see any buildings nearby, not even a barn. Those lights seem to be quite a way off, maybe five kilometres, but it is hard to say," she added.

Tsvetan stood up to his full height and scrabbled up the bank to take a look himself. This confirmed what Tatyana had said and he started to relax a little.

"My intention had been to try and hide the boat," he said, "But there is no cover at all, no bushes, nothing. We cannot just leave it here in case someone finds it and reports it."

Tatyana seemed to think that unlikely. "Surely if someone finds a decent boat like this they would just be glad and keep it," she replied.

Tsvetan was not so sure. "No, fishermen are not like that," he stated adamantly. "Their first question would be, where is the owner and is he safe? It would cause discussion right in the area that we were entering."

Tsvetan thought for a moment and then without further consultation with Tatyana decided to push the boat back into the river. He pushed the old vessel out until the water came above his waist. Believing he was now far enough out to ensure that the boat did not just drift back into the shore he gave it a final shove.

As Milen's boat drifted towards the middle of the river Tsvetan stood motionless in the water watching it bob about until finally it picked up the speed of the river and disappeared into the virtually moonless night. His mind was flooded with memories and his head was for a moment filled with pictures of two young men sitting in the boat laughing and chatting, confident of the futures that awaited them. Before he was ready the picture faded to be brutally replaced by the sight of Milen's body lying in the shallows, the water stained pink by his blood.

With his head lowered and his emotions in pieces Tsvetan turned back towards the shore where the woman he loved waited anxiously. Milen had sacrificed his life to give them this chance. It was a chance that he could not allow to end in tragedy. As he reached the shore he took Tatyana firmly by the hand and with a new determination turned towards the lights of the distant town.

*

At six the next morning Tatyana and Tsvetan walked into the small town that they had believed to be Nikopol, only to find themselves in the much smaller community of Cherkovitsa. The boat had obviously drifted further than they had thought. Although they were both tired, Tsvetan could see danger in lingering in such a small place.

"We must move on, Tatyana. In a place this size everybody knows everyone else. We will be too conspicuous."

Tsvetan had never spent any time in Cherkovitsa before, although he had passed through it on the bus so he knew there was a connection to Pleven. In no time at all they found the bus stop in the centre and with only a drink of water from the village spring to fortify them they boarded the local bus to Pleven. There were only four other passengers on board and they showed no interest in the young couple joining the bus at Cherkovitsa.

At Pleven, with a population of around forty thousand they could blend into the community without drawing any attention to themselves.

"Don't look so sad, Tatyana. When we arrive at Pleven we will get something to eat and plan our next move. You will feel better when you have eaten," Tsvetan assured her. "And don't worry, I have a good feeling about everything. We are just a young Bulgarian couple on a bus to Pleven. We are safe amongst our own."

Tatyana laid her head on Tsvetan's shoulder and smiled up at him. "Whatever you say, husband," she replied feigning marital obedience.

Tsvetan smiled back and although the title had been prematurely bestowed upon him, he decided that 'husband' had rather a nice ring to it.

Less than two hours later Tsvetan and Tatyana were sitting in a small café in Pleven enjoying a cup of coffee and a banitsa with fried potatoes. Tsvetan had been right. With some food inside her Tatyana felt much better and more optimistic.

Nevertheless, it was still more than two hundred kilometres to Plovdiv where Tsvetan hoped they would be able to rest up for a few days. He was pinning his hopes on Mrs Marinova although in truth he did not even know for sure that she was still there. His guess was that she would still be living in the same little house where he had spent several happy years. If she was there he was certain she would help them. He did have one further worry; what if she had another lodger? Nobody trusted anybody else these days and she may be nervous about doing anything too openly. Still, there was no point fretting. He would have all his questions answered soon enough.

"How long do you think it will it take to get to Plovdiv, Tsvetan?" Tatyana asked him.

Tsvetan was immediately conscious that he had more bad news for her and that he would dampen her spirits again, but if they were going to survive, they would both have to be honest.

"I don't know," he replied, "but we must continue to be careful. I don't think we can use trains or even attempt a long bus journey. Remember, I have no papers whatsoever. If we are sitting on a train and a party official or even a ticket inspector asks for our papers we are in big trouble. We must stick to short local journeys by bus where we won't arouse suspicion."

"But that could take forever, Tsvetan," she exclaimed rather loudly causing a few looks from people sitting at nearby tables. Tsvetan was about to admonish her, but could see that she had realised her indiscretion herself. Instead he just concentrated on staying calm. He acknowledged that it would take a while to get to Plovdiv by this means.

"We have no need to hurry. As long as we are careful, getting through Bulgaria should be the easiest part, but we must keep our nerve."

Tatyana felt that she was letting him down and said so. "I am sorry, Tsvetan. I am being foolish and I am relying on you too much. It won't happen again." The apology in her voice and the tears slowly welling up in her beautiful eyes almost broke his heart.

"We can do this, Tanya. We have done it before, returning from Italy. We must believe."

He had never called her Tanya until that moment. This was a pet name that only her mother and occasionally Cleto used. She liked it. Somehow it confirmed that their relationship had changed, become more intimate. Tatyana was determined that she would be strong for him.

"How well do you know the area?" she asked him.

"Not that well," he admitted. "I know that Lovech is about thirty kilometres on from here in the right direction. After that we have to cross the mountains, but I am not sure of the route."

Tatyana was concentrating now. "Do you think buses cross the mountains?" she asked. "Maybe we need to find a route around them."

Tsvetan looked at her with an open expression. He could suddenly sense that he no longer had to protect her.

"To be honest I haven't a clue," he admitted.

"I have an idea," she said. "Let's split up for a bit; couples aren't always together. You can go for a walk and I will go to the bus station and make enquiries. At least I have papers, so if anyone wants to know what I am doing I am safer than you are."

Tsvetan knew this made sense, but was reluctant to split up. If something were to go wrong Tsvetan was worried how they would find each other.

"I don't like the idea of you going on your own," he said, but Tatyana's mind was made up.

"You said yourself we are safe in Bulgaria so long as we are careful. Well, I intend to be very careful," she replied.

Outside the café they kissed briefly and having agreed where to meet they went their separate ways. Within ten minutes Tatyana was at the bus station in the centre of town. First of all she scrutinised the bus timetables, but was completely bamboozled by them and, other than discovering that there was indeed a bus to Plovdiv which they had decided they could not risk taking, she found no information that would help them. Although she had wanted to avoid it she seemed to have no option but to go to the enquiry desk.

Tatyana turned to walk towards the small kiosk and as she did so was immediately confronted by an old poster joyously advertising bus trips across the mountains from Troyan to the famous tourist town of Karlova. Tatyana was captivated by the family depicted on the faded poster. She could be certain that the poster preceded the Communist regime because the family dressed in walking clothes all wore beaming smiles against the backdrop of the mountains rather than the intently serious expressions depicted in modern posters.

An old man sat on a bench facing the poster and was watching Tatyana with a smile spreading across his face.

"I don't expect you remember those days, young lady," he suggested, glad for the opportunity to chat to a pretty young girl.

Tatyana gave him her most winning smile in return. "Unfortunately I don't, although I seem to remember that my parents talked of enjoying their honeymoon in Karlova. Can you still get there by bus?"

The old man was fully engaged now. "There is a bus that goes once or twice a day from Troyan, but it is now a soulless state run service, not very romantic. I doubt your parents would have considered it as a honeymoon." He laughed at the thought. "Lots of people from Troyan work at the rose oil factory in Karlova. The bus is there for them. It leaves pretty early, mind. Those that work in the fields harvest the flowers early in the morning, sometimes before sunrise."

"I might just give it a try, anyway," she cooed, rewarding the old man with another beautiful smile. "How do you get to Troyan?" she enquired, "Is it far?"

"No, not really. If you get a bus to Lovech you can get to Troyan from there, probably about three hours in all."

Tatyana beamed at the dear old man. "I will go and have a look," she announced. "It will be my honeymoon soon. I will demand some rose oil."

They both laughed. Tatyana bent down and gave him a kiss on the forehead.

"Thank you so much. You have made me very happy," she told him and with a girlish wave she turned to go.

"Give the lucky young man my congratulations," he called after her. She promised she would.

Chapter Thirty

"The priest's boat has been found, comrade." The young police sergeant had been despatched to give the news to Vesela Nikolova who had taken personal charge of the man hunt. Vesela received the information apparently without emotion.

"Where?" she asked him.

"I understand it was found early this morning by two fishermen near Cherkovitsa. Their boat was moored there and the priest's boat had become entangled with their moorings. Apparently this suggests the boat had been unmanned at the time."

Vesela looked at him as if he was stupid. "Of course it suggests that," she replied rather impatiently. "Thank you. Goodbye."

The young sergeant hesitated, surprised at his cursory dismissal.

"That will be all, Sergeant Vanchev," she added for the sake of clarity.

Disappointed and slightly bewildered by the poor impression he seemed to have made, the sergeant turned and left.

Vesela sat in her office together with Borislav Martinov, a ruthlessly efficient member of the State Security service from within the Ministry of the Interior. Vesela did not trust him, but on the whole she trusted his judgement.

"The question is where and when did he abandon the boat?" she speculated.

Martinov had already given the matter some thought. "Despite him apparently heading for Romania, given where the boat was found, one can assume he has landed on Bulgarian soil," he replied. "My guess is he landed somewhere and pushed the boat back into the river in the hope it would be carried a long way by the current. Given where it was found he could have come ashore anywhere between the end of Belene Island and Cherkovitsa; where exactly depends on what he had in mind. I assume he would be trying to find fellow Catholics to hide him from the authorities. I will have all known Catholics in the area arrested," Martinov concluded.

"Do that, by all means," Vesela agreed, "But you won't find him that way. I know him. He would not put their lives at risk for his sake. However, if he hears of the arrests he might come forward to prevent it," she said.

Martinov pondered over what Vesela had said. It was true that fugitives could sometimes be flushed out by their concern for others. Useful as this was he deplored their weakness.

"Perhaps we should arrest his family too?" he suggested.

"No!" Vesela's response was emphatic and Martinov lacked the courage to ask why she would not allow this. In truth she was not sure herself, but her thinking quickly moved on.

"He knows he will be putting others at risk if he stays in Bulgaria. My belief is he will try and get back to Italy."

Martinov's reply was verging on disdainful. "That is impossible," he declared. "All borders are closed."

Vesela looked at him indulgently. How naïve these young zealots are, she thought. Did he seriously believe that nobody ever got through the border controls? Twenty leva or a flash of a leg and a promise from a young woman would be enough for many guards to forget their duty, but Borislav Martinov preferred to believe that the borders were impenetrable and the guards loyal. She would allow him to maintain his faith, but Vesela was well aware that crossing the border out of Bulgaria into Greece may be extremely dangerous, but was by no means impossible.

Vesela continued with her own train of thought. "If I am right and he is trying to get through Bulgaria to the West then he will either attempt to stay hidden the whole time, which will be almost impossible, or he will try and mingle with the crowd and that means heading first of all for a town."

Borislav Martinov listened carefully. There was logic in what she was saying.

"So you think he would have headed for Nikopol?" he asked.

"That is my conclusion," she said, getting up from her chair for the first time. "If I am wrong and he wants to remain in Bulgaria then it is only a matter of time until we find him anyway," she added. "I will leave the details to you, Comrade Martinov." The discussion was over.

*

Tatyana was finishing the tale of her conversation with the old man. "And so we have to get a bus from here to Lovech and from there to Troyan. The following morning we can catch the workers' bus to Karlova."

Tsvetan was smiling at her. "And you got all this information from an old man who just happened to be sitting there?" Tsvetan asked her.

"Don't sound so surprised," she objected. "It is easier than you think for me to get my way with men, so just watch out."

Tsvetan laughed. "I have never doubted it."

"Well, we might as well get started," Tatyana suggested. "The old man said he would like to meet you," she added mischievously. "I am sure he will still be there."

Although Tatyana was disappointed that the old man had moved on, Tsvetan was glad. It represented one less complication as far as he was concerned. It was now mid-afternoon and in less than twenty minutes they would be in Lovech. If there was a bus soon Tsvetan saw no reason not to continue on to Troyan. Once there they would have to consider finding somewhere to sleep. His original plan had been to look for a small guest house, but as he thought about it his nerve failed him. So far they had not taken any risks and in a town the size of Troyan a young couple wanting a room for the night was bound to attract attention. These days nobody besides party officials ever travelled anywhere and they would have to come up with some elaborate tale about where they were travelling from and where they were going. Also it was probable that guest houses were required to keep details of people that stayed with them and he had nothing to show by way of identity papers.

Tatyana seemed to be reading his thoughts. "We will have to sleep soon, otherwise we will be exhausted. I am dog tired now," she said.

"I know," Tsvetan replied. "I am just not sure where we should go."

"When we get to Troyan we should have something to eat and when it is dark leave town and find somewhere, an old barn, an animal shelter, a shepherd's hut, anything. It doesn't matter."

This was Tatyana's view and Tsvetan had no difficulty in agreeing.

"Yes, you are right. As long as we don't leave any trace that we have been there," he replied.

"Remind me not to leave a thank you note then," she quipped. Tsvetan gave her arm an affectionate squeeze. It was clear now that Tatyana had regained her spirit.

*

The café owner in Pleven watched as the two officers went across the road to another café. He was sure he recognised the man in the photograph that the security police had shown him. He only remembered him because of the pretty girl that was with him. She was not a classic beauty, but had something about her that had made the proprietor notice her, would make any man notice her. However, he had kept a deadpan face and said emphatically that he had never seen the man before. The security police had said he was a dangerous criminal, a description he heard so often that he had come to doubt its validity. He was probably just another poor soul that had got on the wrong side of the authorities. Anyway, his approach in these matters was well entrenched: don't get involved.

Borislav Martinov and his team had got nowhere in Nikopol and had decided to move south in the general direction of the Greek border, but Martinov needed some kind of lead. He would never find the priest like this. Anyway, he was aware that most people would keep quiet even if they did recognise the man in the picture his team were trailing around the cafes and bars.

He needed something more concrete. He looked again at the hopeless profile he had been given of Father Tsvetan Viktorov by the authorities at Belene Island. It dealt almost entirely with the priest's supposed crimes and sedition, most of which was probably nonsense and said nothing about the man himself. Then he noticed near the beginning of the document a passing reference to the fact that he had studied in Plovdiv.

Martinov called one of his assistants over and told him to open the map showing Bulgaria and its neighbouring states. Plovdiv was due south from Nikopol and little more than a hundred kilometres from the border with Greece. The priest would have friends in the town. Martinov felt sure he would have headed there. With a new sense of purpose he gathered his men together and gave the order to drive at once to Plovdiv.

Chapter Thirty One

This time Cleto could do nothing to alleviate the depression into which his wife had sunk. He had returned from work to find that Tatyana was gone. Her mother would not say where she was. She insisted that she did not know her daughter's whereabouts, but Cleto could tell that she did know. He could get no sense from her, barely a coherent sentence. In his despair he had called in his friend and neighbour, Dr Filipov, but this had turned out to be a mistake. Yordana had become so agitated by Dr Filipov's attempt at interviewing her that the good doctor had been forced to withdraw.

"I don't know what to suggest, Cleto. Clearly she is upset by the disappearance of her daughter. I can only put it down to that," Dr Filipov concluded.

Cleto was not so sure. "Of course it is a factor, but it is more than that. There is something she is not telling me about Tanya. She knows something I am certain," Cleto replied. He was feeling absolutely desperate.

The very next day an over-excited Dr Filipov called on Cleto again.

"Cleto, my son has rung from the hospital. A colleague has today been treating a senior official from Belene Island Labour Camp. He told his surgeon that they had experienced their first ever successful escape. Apparently they got a tip off at the last minute, but it was too late and the prisoner still got away. Cleto, it was Father Viktorov."

Cleto was dumbstruck. Tatyana must have known beforehand. She had gone to join him.

"There is no other explanation," he murmured, more to himself than to the doctor.

"What do you mean, Cleto? No other explanation? What are you saying?"

Cleto looked up as if he had only just become aware that there was someone else in the room. His passionate eyes were full of tears, his loving heart full of fear.

174

"She is with him. She must be with him. It is the only explanation."

Dr Filipov put his arm around his friend's shoulder in a forlorn attempt to comfort him. He remembered Cleto's joy when his wife returned from the camp and soon after his beloved stepdaughter came home as well. He had never known his friend so happy and relieved, as if he had been rescued from a nightmare. The two men had celebrated with a bottle of Pinot Nero. Now Cleto's world had fallen apart again and this time the doctor doubted if it could be put back together.

*

Once in Plovdiv Martinov's first port of call was the university.

"I must say, I find all of this very hard to believe," said the Vice-Chancellor displaying a dangerous level of candour given who he was speaking to. "I remember Tsvetan Viktorov very well. He was one of our best students. The idea that he has become a dangerous and subversive criminal beggars belief."

Borislav Martinov had already heard more than he wanted to hear from this overpaid academic. He was rapidly losing his patience.

"Vice-Chancellor, I am not the least bit interested in your opinion of Viktorov, even less your sentimental recollections about him. He is a known criminal and a traitor to Bulgaria. He has escaped from Belene Island Prison Camp. Once found he will be executed. I would seriously advise you to cooperate with our enquiries otherwise you might be seeing the inside of a labour camp yourself." Martinov paused to allow the Vice-Chancellor to take in what he had said and then continued, barking out his orders. "I want everything you know about him: who his friends were, the church he attended, where he lived when in Plovdiv and so on. Do I make myself clear?"

The Vice-Chancellor knew he was on dangerous ground, but remained for the time being defiant.

"I do not have all the details you ask for and any information we do hold here at the university is of course confidential."

With just a glance from Martinov, his assistant moved swiftly. He took hold of the Vice-Chancellor's wrist pinning it to the desk and, staring him in the eye as he did so, he slowly extinguished his cigarette on the back of the man's hand. The Vice-Chancellor winced with the pain.

"So if you could be so kind?" Martinov continued.

The Vice-Chancellor lifted the phone and summoned his secretary who appeared almost immediately from the adjoining room.

"Miss Bakalova, could you please bring me the file for Tsvetan Viktorov. He graduated from here in 1941."

"Yes, I remember him well," she trilled. Then, rapidly taking in the scene before her, Miss Bakalova rushed off to comply with the instructions she had been given. Within a few minutes she was back. She placed the file in front of her boss, but Martinov unceremoniously snatched up the manila folder from the desk and immediately started rifling through it. Miss Bakalova looked on in horror at the disrespect being shown to the Vice-Chancellor. Not knowing how to react she looked at her boss for guidance. He smiled at her affectionately. They had worked together for a long time and the loyalty cut both ways.

"That will be all, Miss Bakalova. Thank you," he said and with uncertain steps she left the room.

Silence prevailed as Martinov rapidly took in the details from the file. Eventually he spoke.

"This is a start, but I need more, much more. My assistant will be back later today for more information from you. I advise you not to disappoint him."

Martinov's assistant gave the Vice-Chancellor an odious smile. "We will meet again later," he confirmed.

By far the most useful piece of information in the university's file was the address where he had lived as a student. There were also documents and references indicating that he had taken up a teaching post in the city after graduating and had apparently continued to live at the same digs. The home of Mrs Marinova would be their next stop.

*

By taking only short bus journeys from one town to another Tatyana and Tsvetan had finally reached Plovdiv without incident. Tsvetan was sure the authorities would be looking for him, but whether they realised he was accompanied he could not be sure. He knew he had been betrayed and by whom, but how much Yordana knew and how much she had passed on he could not tell. Also he had no idea how far Milen's old boat had floated before it was either seen on the river with no one aboard or drifted into the bank. He could only hope that it had gone a fair distance and not betrayed where they had landed. What he could not have known was that Vesela Nikolova had accurately worked out his plan. Now that he was at last in Plovdiv he felt a degree safer, but at the same time realised that he still needed to exercise considerable care. Also as he got nearer to Mrs Marinova's house his anxieties about her no longer being there returned.

"What if she is not there, Tatyana? What then? I have not been in touch with her for years. I don't even know for sure if she is still alive."

Tatyana had been having the same doubts and on top of that she did not feel certain that the woman would help them. It was clear that Tsvetan and his ex-landlady were very fond of each other, but since the time that Tsvetan had lived here everything in Bulgaria had changed. Many people lived in fear of the new regime and would be reluctant to help anyone that was on the run, even someone they had great affection for. However, she could see that for the first time Tsvetan was feeling anxious and under pressure and this was not the time to express her own concerns.

"She will be there, Tsvetan. From what you have told me about her she does not sound like the type of woman that would just uproot herself. After all, you said it is the house she shared with her husband. She would not leave it now when everything else in Bulgaria is so uncertain. She will be there."

Tsvetan took some comfort from Tatyana's confidence. "You are right, Tatyana. It is just that the closer we get the more nervous I become."

177

Tatyana kissed him on the cheek and squeezed his hand. He smiled back at her, but it was not a convincing smile. Tatyana decided that their next move should be down to her.

"When we are close enough for you to direct me I think I should go to the house alone," she announced.

Tsvetan shook his head in disbelief. "Why would we do that?" he asked her. "You don't even know her and she can be wary of strangers."

Tatyana had her reasons for this suggestion and held firm. "When I tell her who I am she will not see me as a stranger."

"But why, Tanya? Surely we should stay together."

"What if the authorities have already been to see her?" Tatyana replied. "It is likely that they have been paying visits to almost everyone that knows you."

"But they think I headed to Romania," he insisted.

"You wanted them to think that and they would have contacted the Romanian authorities, but just as you worked out that Romania was not a good option, they would have realised that too. You are the first person ever to escape from that wretched place, Tsvetan. They will do anything to find you."

Tsvetan was slowly understanding her logic. He realised how naïve he had been and at the same moment it occurred to him that they would have paid a visit to his parents. He was causing heartache and real danger for everyone. The sooner they got out of Bulgaria the better.

"I have changed my mind. We cannot go to Mrs Marinova. It is asking too much of her. We could be putting her life in danger." Tsvetan was adamant. It was as if he had suddenly woken up to the realities of life in Communist Bulgaria. "Somehow we will have to get to Greece without any help from friends."

"If we must do it alone, then we will," Tatyana replied.

From where they stood he could see the turning into Bogomil Street. He realised that he was giving up the opportunity for them both to rest for a few days, get cleaned up and summon the energy for the final and hardest stretch of their journey. Nevertheless it was out of the question. To gain his freedom his best friend was dead and his school friend Dido could be too. He would not put someone else at risk.

Suddenly as they stood there thinking what to do next they heard the sound of a car coming along the street behind them. The large black limousine flew past them and turned into Bogomil Street, the wheels screeching as the car took the corner too fast. Instinctively Tsvetan ran the short distance to the start of the street. He could see number thirty seven clearly. Nothing had changed. As he watched, four men in black jackets got out of the car and walked briskly towards the front door of number thirty seven, no doubt treading on the vegetables that would be spilling over the edge of the path. He wanted to wait and see Mrs Marinova standing in the doorway asking them their business, but a hand tore at his arm.

"Tsvetan, come on, run!" In an instant he recovered from the trance into which he had fallen and with memories of another life pounding in his brain he turned and fled.

Chapter Thirty Two

"We have interviewed his landlady from his time in Plovdiv and we are now checking out friends and church people that he knew, but I am not hopeful. The Marinova woman said she had not seen him since he left the city years ago and I tend to believe her. We searched the house, but there was no sign of anyone staying there or having been there. My men will be speaking to other contacts today, but my instinct tells me he has not been in Plovdiv at all."

On the other end of the phone line Vesela Nikolova was thinking through the options. She had been impressed by Martinov's hunch regarding Plovdiv, but it looked as if the trail was cold.

"I am still sure that he is aiming to get into Greece," she told Martinov. "If we have failed to cut him off on the way then we need to make sure we are ready at the border. The question is where will he try and cross."

Martinov was one step ahead of her. "A large part of the border crosses the Eastern Rhodope Mountains. Except for the Makaza pass near Kirkovo it would be almost impossible to cross. The pass is closed and heavily guarded. The border guards have been alerted, but I can't see him trying that."

"What about the border between Zlatograd and Thermes?" Vesela asked him.

"That is a possibility." Martinov's reply indicated that he had already thought of that too. "Again I have alerted the guards there. If he tries that we will be ready for him."

Vesela had been struck before by Martinov's complete faith in the efficiency of the guards. She remained sceptical. "Are you sure these guards can be relied on?" she asked.

"I have told the officers in charge of each crossing that if he gets past them then they will be held personally responsible. I think they both know what that means."

Vesela could herself be tough when required, but she found Martinov's ruthlessness quite chilling. This reminded her of something she had been meaning to say to him.

"You can tell them as well, Martinov, that I want him alive. I will not be happy if they deliver a corpse to me. Is that clear?" It was clear enough, although privately Martinov could not see why it mattered.

"I will tell them, comrade," he replied.

"There is one more possibility," Martinov continued. "Crossings at the border near Chepintsi, south of Rudozem have been attempted recently by a number of East Germans. They travel to Bulgaria on holiday and then try to get out from Chepintsi."

"Have they succeeded?" Vesela asked.

"More than sixty people have been shot dead," Martinov told her proudly.

"That is not what I asked," she responded impatiently.

"There are no records of anyone succeeding," he replied. Vesela took this last piece of information with a pinch of salt.

"Are the East German authorities aware of this?" she asked.

"Yes, I understand that the Bulgarian border guards are defending this crossing point with the active engagement of the East German secret police."

Vesela was clear that if the Stasi were involved the crossing was more likely to be secure. She replaced the receiver and not for the first time tried to get into Tsvetan's mind. She recalled her late husband's diaries that showed quite clearly how much he admired the young Tsvetan. The one time she had met him he had made her feel quite uncomfortable with his quiet strength. Despite her own discomfort during that meeting, she could not help but be impressed. The camp at Belene was an appalling place and she felt sure that life there was almost intolerable, but when she offered him a way out he did not consider it, even for a moment. Then there was his friend Milen. He was without doubt a true believer in the Communist cause and the young man had a bright future ahead of him. Nevertheless, he had without hesitation put his friendship with the young priest above everything and had paid with his life. Father Tsvetan Viktorov was clearly a very remarkable man.

Vesela opened her desk drawer to take out a map. As well as the map the drawer contained a few personal items, some documents waiting for her signature and a photograph of her late husband. This photograph had stood on her desk in a small modest frame for several years, but since his death she had found it painful to look at. It was as if he was rebuking her for her disregard for his welfare. He had died without even knowing her whereabouts or the reason she had left. In some small way she felt a debt to Tsvetan who had at least provided some friendship to Slavko in his later years.

Vesela pushed the photograph aside and picked up the map. She wanted to be clear exactly where the different border crossings spoken of by Martinov were located. She tended to agree with Martinov's assertion that Father Viktorov would not be able to cross the mountains other than through the Makaza pass. The man had been half starved at the labour camp and his reserves of energy and general fitness would have been severely compromised. The idea of him trying to cross the mountains other than on an established route was not realistic.

Vesela studied the map and saw at once that the border near Chepintsi was not only the nearest to Plovdiv by a considerable margin, but was also due south from Nikopol where she still assumed he had started from. A man in his condition would surely take the easiest route. He would of course know nothing about the presence of the East German Stasi at this border point. She was sure this was his destination.

She picked up the phone again and asked to be re-connected to Borislav Martinov.

"Comrade Martinov, please get one of your men to pick me up and take me to the border crossing at Chepintsi. I am sure Father Viktorov is heading there. I intend to take personal charge of his capture."

Martinov had come to the same conclusion regarding the priest's intended destination.

"I will pick you up myself," he offered.

"No, you and the remainder of your team should continue looking in Plovdiv. Even if he is heading for the border at Chepintsi we don't know when he will get there. He could easily still be in Plovdiv."

Martinov started to object. "I am sure he is no longer there. I believe...."

"Those are my orders, Comrade," Vesela interjected and with that she replaced the receiver.

*

Other than to eat something, Tsvetan and Tatyana did not want to stay in Plovdiv any longer than necessary. They were both unnerved by the ease with which the authorities had traced them to the city. As a result they were unsure what to do next.

"They must have found the boat close to where we left it," said Tatyana. "How else would they have worked out where we were heading?" she added.

"You are probably right," Tsvetan confirmed, "But it makes no difference now. The question is where to next. My view is that we should head for Rudozem and from there to the crossing at Chepintsi. It is where we entered last year so at least we have some knowledge of the area."

Tatyana was losing her nerve altogether now. She was starting to believe that whatever they did the authorities would know.

"I am frightened, Tsvetan. What if they are waiting for us there?"

Tatyana was obsessively sucking her hair and occasionally scratching her forehead, two nervous habits that she had completely conquered several years earlier, but which were now returning as a result of the anxiety she was feeling. Tsvetan watched her and felt an overwhelming guilt. Their problems were not of her making. He took her hand and held her close. He was on the verge of saying that she should return home, but he knew it would be a hollow gesture. She would not consider it for a moment and would probably feel undermined by the suggestion. Whatever toll it was taking on them, Tsvetan realised they were in this together, whatever the outcome.

Still unable to come up with a plan that they could believe in, Tatyana and Tsvetan had found a deserted barn just outside the city and slept there for two nights trying to work out what to do next.

It was now Sunday and as they skulked around the city with Tatyana frightened by every shadow, Tsvetan made a decision. In his early years at Plovdiv he and Mrs Marinova had made a habit of eating at a particular restaurant every Sunday. It was a simple place serving the best traditional Bulgarian food. More often than not they had been joined by her late husband's sister, Rumena. For some reason that he had never really understood one Sunday Mrs Marinova had announced that she no longer wished to eat there and in future she would eat at home. Rumena had suspected that she had fallen out with the proprietor's wife whom they had both known since childhood.

"They were always falling out at school," Rumena had told him. "Sometimes it lasted for months. It will blow over."

Unfortunately it never did and although for a while Tsvetan doggedly carried on the tradition he never enjoyed it so much alone. After a while he reverted to eating at home with Mrs Marinova who never mentioned the restaurant again. Before they left the city like two fugitives he and Tatyana would eat there together like two civilised people. He put the suggestion to Tatyana who thought the idea insane.

"No, Tsvetan, we must get away. They are looking for us. They may come there."

Tsvetan had made up his mind. "It is a big city Tatyana and there is absolutely no reason why they would be looking for us at that restaurant. There are hundreds like it in Plovdiv," he replied. "Up until now we have kept safe by mingling with the crowds in each town and city we have passed through. We will have a simple meal there and then we will head for Rudozem," he said, suddenly decisive. "If they find us then so be it. We must trust in God."

Chapter Thirty Three

"There is nothing to compare with a Bulgarian restaurant on a Sunday," said Tatyana who had enjoyed the tradition of eating out on a Sunday afternoon for most of her life.

She was now so glad that she had allowed Tsvetan to persuade her and she could feel herself relaxing despite the dangers. At most tables there were families represented by several generations with grandparents indulging their grandchildren while the parents feigned disapproval of what their kids were getting away with. Tatyana smiled at Tsvetan as she hoped with all her heart that they would survive their current ordeal and live to raise a family of their own.

"Maybe this will be us in a few years," she suggested.

"I do not doubt it," he replied defying the odds. "We have got this far, Tanya, we will get to Greece. I am certain of it."

Tsvetan froze as he felt the hand on his shoulder. He was terrified to look round, but when he finally summoned the courage to do so he was confronted by the smiling face of Mrs Marinova's sister-in-law, Rumena. It took him a while to recover himself and for his heart to stop pounding like a steam hammer. When he finally came to he stood up so abruptly that he knocked a chair over in his eagerness to greet his old friend. The restauranteur looked across and Tsvetan worried that he had attracted unwelcome notice, but soon the man's stern demeanour turned to a smile as he realised that he was witnessing nothing more than an unexpected reunion.

"Tsvetan, I can't believe it is you. It is wonderful to see you, but…" As she spoke the smile drained from her face to be replaced by a look of concern. "You must know the authorities are looking for you?" she said.

Tsvetan nodded. "Yes, I know." For the time being this was all he said. He was anxious to hear what she knew.

"Iva Marinova has had a visit from the security police. They searched the house looking for any trace of you, but of course they found nothing. You had not been there." Tsvetan did not tell her that at the time he was only a few metres from the house.

"Iva is in a terrible state. She would want to help you, but she had no idea where you were. Perhaps it is just as well," said Rumena.

"Yes, it was better that she knew nothing," Tsvetan confirmed.

Just at that moment Tatyana came out of the restaurant toilet where she had been struggling to wash her face and do something with her hair. She saw that Tsvetan was on his feet. At first she was frightened, but it soon became clear to her that he was talking to someone he knew. Not certain what to do she held back, but when Tsvetan saw her he called her over. Rumena looked round as she approached, not sure what to make of the sudden appearance of a young woman and a pretty one at that, despite the worry lines across her face. She turned back to Tsvetan.

"I don't understand. They referred to you as Father Viktorov, a Catholic priest."

Tsvetan looked intently into her eyes. "I am a Catholic priest, but there is too much to explain. Rumena, we need help and quickly. Can you help us?"

Rumena did not hesitate. "Of course I will help if I can. What can I do?"

In a low voice and as succinctly as possible Tsvetan described their plight and outlined their plan to get to Greece via Rudozem, although when he listened to himself it did not sound much like a plan. Rumena listened anxiously, but it was slowly becoming clear to her that by some miracle she could indeed help them.

"Tsvetan, my son knows of a group that helps East German dissidents get out through Bulgaria. He is not part of it although he does support it. I worry about him, but he says we must all do what we can to try and oppose this Communist nightmare."

"East Germans?" exclaimed Tsvetan, not sure how or why this should be.

"Yes, it has become almost impossible to get from East Germany directly into the West. As a consequence a new route through Bulgaria has opened up, although the Stasi have unfortunately become aware of it. They are often present there alongside the Bulgarian guards."

Tsvetan had believed that God would find a way. Perhaps this was it, but with the infamous Stasi also guarding the crossing it sounded more dangerous than ever. He expressed this fear to Rumena.

"It is dangerous I am sure, but they do have some system for getting people across," she said. "For obvious reasons they do not share this information widely."

Up until now Tatyana had remained quiet, but she was fast coming to the conclusion that this could be the opportunity they had been praying for.

"Tsvetan, we must take any help offered. At this moment we have no idea how we would otherwise get across."

Tsvetan nodded his agreement. "You are right, Tanya." And then turning to Rumena he asked, "What do we do next?"

Rumena herself did not know any details. "You must meet with my son Georgi as soon as possible," she replied.

They had now been in the restaurant for quite a long time. Tatyana and indeed Rumena were getting nervous.

"Tsvetan, suggest a place where we could meet with Georgi," Tatyana said. "We must move on."

Tsvetan was trying to think of somewhere that any person from Plovdiv would know, but that was not too conspicuous. "The small cafe at the entrance to Stoyan Chalukov Street, down the hill from the Roman Amphitheatre," he suggested.

Rumena agreed. "Be there in an hour," she said. "I will go and tell him now. And be careful!"

They parted without fuss and soon Tsvetan and Tatyana were sitting in the little cafe nervously looking at each person as they entered.

"Hello, my dears, how are you?" said an elderly lady as she came in.

Tatyana gave her a smile and a mumbled greeting. She then turned and addressed Tsvetan. "We must be more careful. We were looking at her so intently she thought she knew us. We must stop doing that."

"I will just look at your lovely face," he replied in an attempt to lighten the mood, but it went down like a lead balloon.

"Don't patronise me, Tsvetan. I look an absolute sight. You know I do."

Tsvetan was taken aback. It was probably the first harsh words from Tatyana since their ordeal began. "Don't be silly," he said and was about to try and put matters right between them when the door into the cafe opened again. Despite what had just been said both sets of eyes turned to look at the newcomers.

The two men were large and imposing in their black coats and trousers. They were unmistakeably from the State Security. Tsvetan and Tatyana looked at each other trying not to show the terror they were both feeling. Getting up to leave was impossible, they both knew that. They would just have to see it out. Tsvetan reached forward to take her hand, but she instinctively withdrew it and immediately regretted her actions. However, the two men paid little attention to the guests. Instead they went directly to the man behind the counter. The younger of the two men reached into his coat pocket and pulled out a photograph. From where she sat Tatyana could see the man shaking his head emphatically.

"Are you sure you have not seen him?" he was asked, but again he shook his head and said he had not.

"I only work here two days per week," he said. "The old lady over there, Mrs Isaeva. She comes here almost every day. You could ask her."

The younger officer looked round and saw the elderly woman sitting alone by the window. It did not look promising, he thought. The two men sauntered over to the table and again the younger man pulled the picture of Tsvetan out of his coat pocket.

"Baba, have you seen this man anywhere?"

The woman studied it carefully. "No, I haven't seen him. I wish I had. He is rather cute," she observed.

The state security officer grinned. "A bit young for you, I would have thought," he said.

"When you get to my age no one is either too young or too old," she replied and as if to emphasise the point she gave his buttocks a quick squeeze.

"You dirty old bugger!" he protested.

His older colleague laughed at him. "Don't be so proud, comrade. The time will come when you will be glad to take up such an offer."

The older man took back the photograph and handed it to his partner. They left with the older man still laughing and his comrade wondering what was so funny.

It felt to Tsvetan as if he had not breathed from the moment the two men entered the bar. Tatyana was as white as a sheet. Before they could decide whether to say anything to the woman, she spoke to them.

"Wait a few minutes and then leave," she told them. "Luckily for you the State Security like to employ the most stupid of people because they are more likely to do exactly as they are told. It is unlikely they will come back, but if they do we are all dead, including the barman," she added with authority.

Tsvetan looked at her, unsure what if anything to share with her. Tatyana had no such reservations.

"We must stay. We are meeting someone," she said, her lower lip trembling with anxiety.

"I know," the old woman informed her, "But Georgi is not important now. You need to leave at once. At the other end of this street there is an old bus shelter. Be there at exactly five o clock tomorrow morning. You will be picked up by a meat wagon and taken beyond Rudozem."

Tsvetan opened his mouth to speak, but the old woman raised her hand for silence.

"No questions now. I hope you are not squeamish. He is taking the meat from the city abattoir to the markets in and around Rudozem. You will travel in the back with the fresh carcasses." She allowed herself a thin smile. "May God go with you!" she said finally and turned her back on them.

Chapter Thirty Four

From inside the back of the meat wagon Tsvetan and Tatyana could see nothing, not even each other. Each time the lorry stopped they hoped they had reached their destination only for the wagon to rumble forward again. This time, however, they heard the engine being switched off and shortly afterwards there was the sound of footsteps outside. To their relief they could hear the driver fumbling with the lock and a few seconds later the back door at last swung open. With a wave of an arm the driver ushered them out.

"You have survived I see," he observed with a muted smile.

"We are just so grateful for your help," Tsvetan replied.

The driver shrugged off the thanks and got straight down to business. "You will wait in that barn across the road. You needn't worry about the farmer. He is a friend to us. Just wait there until someone comes for you to take you across the border."

Tsvetan and Tatyana looked incredulous. The driver made it sound straightforward.

Accurately reading their thoughts, he continued. "It is of course dangerous for all of us, but we have a system that seems to work for now. Usually we take East Germans, but if anything it should be easier with Bulgarians'," he told them.

Tsvetan was curious. "How has it come about that you take mainly East Germans?" he asked.

The driver shrugged his shoulders. "We do it for the money." he said simply. "They are not normal dissidents, they are high ranking officials in the German Communist Party disillusioned with how things are working out. They come to Bulgaria on holiday with the purpose of escaping into the west. They pay well."

"One of your colleagues told us that the Stasi know about this. Is that so?"

The driver was reluctant to answer so many questions. He had more pressing things to tell them. "They know which border they are passing through, but they don't know how," he replied. "Now listen, let's go across to the barn and I will tell you what you need to know."

Sat in the barn on bales of straw, Tsvetan and Tatyana listened carefully as the driver explained how they get people through.

"Several times a week trucks pass across this border into Greece to buy luxury items for members of the Bulgarian Politburo. The drivers are genuine, but those accompanying them are often people fleeing the East like yourselves. They travel openly in the cab. The drivers and the guards are badly paid. It has proved very easy to bribe them with East German Marks. The guards take a cursory look at their papers and let them through."

Tsvetan interrupted the driver. "I don't have any papers," he told him anxiously.

The driver looked at him with indulgence. "I have papers for each of you here," he said.

Before he could conclude Tatyana also had a question. "Is it normal to have women in the cab?"

Like most men the driver was captivated by the girl. He was considerably more patient with regard to her questions than those posed by Tsvetan. "Yes it is very normal," he told her. "The Politburo wives prefer women to make the trip. They trust them more to buy the items they want. You will not be conspicuous."

He continued with their instructions. "Now you will wait here until the truck that is going to take you across picks you up. Remember, the driver is not part of our movement, so don't ask him or tell him anything. You can make polite conversation; that is all. He will be glad you are Bulgarians. He will worry less at the border."

He handed them each their papers. "Read them carefully so you know who you are," he instructed them. With a smile intended mainly for Tatyana, he turned to leave. "Good luck!" he called as he left the barn.

*

Borislav Martinov was annoyed and frustrated that he had been ordered to continue the search in Plovdiv. He had long since concluded that the priest was no longer there and could not understand that Vesela Nikolova had insisted he stay. It was absurd that she did not want him at the border. Finding escaped fugitives was his bread and butter business. Surely this was outside Comrade Nikolova's experience, he thought.

Martinov had for some time been investigating the means by which East Germans were getting across the border at Chepintsi. He believed that if they could solve this then the border would be more secure and they would in turn be more likely to catch the priest. Also it irked him that nationals from other countries were using Bulgarian borders to escape in the belief they were easier to cross. He knew that the East German Stasi held their Bulgarian counterparts in contempt and this angered him. He had not told Vesela Nikolova, but it was estimated that several hundred East Germans had over the last year gone on holiday to Bulgaria and not returned. A significant number of these had almost certainly escaped to the West.

Some had been caught, but these were the ones who just made a desperate attempt to cut their way through the border fence and sneak across the wide area of 'no man's land' between the fence and the Greek border. Stopping them was easy. Those that had crossed successfully almost certainly had help from local Bulgarians who were hostile to the Communist regime. Also he would not be surprised if some of the border guards were complicit. Martinov called one of his men into the office who he remembered had previously been a border guard before joining the State Security service. He explained what he was trying to find out.

"Do you think it possible that some of the border guards are involved in this?" he asked him.

"To be blunt, comrade, some of them would sell their own daughters to get enough cash for cigarettes and rakia and I have little doubt that these Germans pay handsomely," his colleague replied.

"But how would they do it? How could they let them through right under the nose of the Stasi?" Martinov wondered.

"I don't know. Perhaps they travel with the legitimate consignments?" he suggested.

Martinov was interested in this possibility. "So what are the legitimate consignments?" Martinov asked. "I thought they turned everyone back."

The man did not know how much information to give to his boss, but finally decided it was in his best interests to be seen as helpful by Martinov. "Well, in spite of the official embargo on goods travelling between Bulgaria and the West, there is still a lot of trade with Greece and there are trucks carrying goods in both directions. It is not as much as before the borders were closed, but it is still significant."

Borislav Martinov was of the view that any trade with the West would only undermine the Communist model. More than that he believed it opened up real security risks. He was a senior member of the State Security service so how come he was not aware of this? Obviously he was not meant to know.

"So who authorises this trade with Greece?" he asked his officer.

"I am not sure. It has always been so. I think it is an informal agreement between the Politburo and the Border Agency."

Martinov did not like what he was hearing, although he knew that if this was at the behest of the Politburo he would have to be careful. One thing he did know was that he had authority over any member of the Border Agency especially where security was involved.

He picked up his phone. "I want to speak to a senior member of the Border Agency, whoever is in charge of the border with Greece. I don't have a name. Find out who it is and a few details about him, before you put me through." He put down the receiver.

Ten minutes later his phone rang. Martinov was told that the head of the Southern Border Force was a man named Petar Dimov. Apparently he was only thirty one and was new in post. "Put me through," said Martinov.

*

"I don't think I could ever eat meat again," Tatyana maintained. "A few times as we went round a sharp bend a carcass brushed against me. It was horrible."

Having spent a long period of time in a Communist labour camp, being asked to travel in the back of a meat wagon was not something Tsvetan viewed as a hardship. However, he kept his thoughts to himself. He gave Tatyana an affectionate hug.

"By tomorrow it will all be over," he assured her.

"Yes, one way or another," she replied.

Tsvetan held her tighter. "We must remain positive, Tanya. We will get to Greece. I am sure of it."

They sat down again on the bale of straw to wait for the truck. They both hoped it would not be for too long.

*

Petar Dimov was nervous when told that there was a call from Borislav Martinov. Martinov was well known as a ruthless State Security commander. Dimov was already aware that Martinov had gone over his head and given orders as well as threats to his staff at the border posts near Zlatograd and at the Makaza pass. He wished that he had objected at the time, but it was too late now. After a short pause to gather himself he took the call.

"Comrade Dimov, I hope you can help me. I am pursuing a criminal who recently escaped from Belene Island Prison Camp. I believe he is heading for the border with Greece just beyond Chepintsi. I have been told this border post comes under your jurisdiction."

Dimov confirmed that this was the case. Martinov continued. "I have learned that informal trade still exists between our country and Greece and that the consignments pass through the Chepintsi border. Is this so?"

Dimov hesitated for a split second, long enough for Martinov to pounce. "Dimov, I know already this is the case. I want the fullest information about it. I trust we understand each other." Dimov understood. "How many trucks pass through each day?" Martinov asked.

"Not many," replied Dimov, "I would say about ten or fifteen per week leave Bulgaria and a similar number come to us from Greece."

Martinov pondered for a moment. This was less than he expected. Surely it was possible to thoroughly search such a small number of trucks.

"The drivers going towards Greece, are they accompanied?" he asked.

Dimov was adamant. "No they are alone. My guards thoroughly check their papers and spend up to an hour with each vehicle checking their cargo. I am confident that the border is secure," he maintained.

Martinov treated this assertion with contempt. "That is a dangerous boast, comrade, when we both know that East Germans are regularly escaping through your so-called border controls. Why else would the Stasi have a presence there?"

Petar Dimov was worried now. "Comrade Martinov, I don't think…"

"I am not interested in what you think," Martinov interrupted. "Are they the only vehicles that cross the border?"

Dimov was now starting to believe that Martinov knew the answers to his own questions. He would have to be careful how he replied. "Well yes, except for our own patrol vehicles." Dimov hesitated for a moment as a thought occurred to him. "Except of course the small trucks collecting luxury goods for senior Politburo members."

There was a hesitation on the line as the two men simultaneously reached the same conclusion. Martinov was the first to speak.

"Please tell me these drivers are not accompanied," he said.

"They are only accompanied by staff chosen and vetted by Politburo members, people that they trust," Dimov replied weakly.

"And you check this, how?" Martinov asked him and was met at first with silence.

Dimov cleared his throat that had become choked by anxiety. "I will personally go to the border and ensure that proper checks are done."

Martinov jumped on him like a panther. "You will go nowhere, comrade!" he ordered. "You will remain exactly where you are until you are relieved of your position," he added with venom. "I will go myself." Martinov slammed down the phone and stuck his head through the adjoining door of his office. "Get me a car immediately!" he yelled.

*

As the truck that would take them across the border drew up outside the old barn, Vesela Nikolova had already arrived at the border point to which they were heading. About thirty minutes behind them, driving like a lunatic was Borislav Martinov. Tsvetan followed the instructions they had been given attempting to involve the driver only in conversation similar to what passes between people waiting for a bus or sat outside a doctor's surgery. However, even this failed to engage the driver and soon silence descended on the cab with each of the three people consumed with their own thoughts and separate anxieties.

Recently the driver had promised his wife that he would stop carrying these passengers, but he earned more than his monthly salary in one trip and was continuing without her knowledge. It was easy work, but he was at all times aware that if it went wrong he would face imprisonment or even execution. Perhaps he would make this trip the last, he thought.

After less than twenty minutes Tsvetan and Tatyana could see the border post ahead.

"Don't speak unless spoken to," the driver told them and again fell silent. As they drove towards the barrier it stayed down and the driver stopped in front of it. As the guard approached the vehicle, Tatyana could hear her own pulse throbbing in her ears. Tsvetan looked out of the window saying a silent prayer. Up until now all had been answered. He wondered if their luck would hold.

At the guard's request the driver got out of the cab and opened the back of the truck. As expected it was empty.

"What do our lords and masters want you to bring them this time?" the guard asked him.

"The usual," he replied, "Chocolate, perfume, ouzo, French cognac, new outfits for the wives and girlfriends; my two passengers know exactly what to get."

The guard smiled. "Best get going then." he suggested. "We don't want to keep them waiting. I just need to check the papers of your two friends and you can be on your way."

The driver climbed aboard and told Tsvetan and Tatyana to produce their documents. He handed them to the guard who took a cursory look at them and returned them.

"Ok, through you go," he said.

The driver started the engine and was about to put his truck into gear when a woman called from behind for him to stop. Tsvetan looked in the wing mirror and saw Vesela Nikolova flanked by two Stasi officers approaching the vehicle. He thought of grabbing Tatyana and making a run for it, but they would be shot before they even got out of the lorry.

"You have not properly scrutinised their papers," said Vesela looking at the guard with contempt. "Give them to me."

The guard stood more erect and in a more formal manner again requested their identity documents. He handed them to Vesela who checked them herself before sharing them with her East German colleagues. They returned them to her and she asked Tatyana a few questions about herself. Tatyana tried not to show the terror she was feeling. Although she had memorised the information contained in the documents, the one thing she could not recall was her assumed name. The relief when the papers were handed back to her was palpable.

"You, look at me!" she shouted to Tsvetan. He turned to face her believing this to be where it all came to an end. "Where are you from?" she asked him.

"From Sofia," he replied "Parchevich Street."

"And your mother's maiden name?" Vesela continued.

"Minkova." he confirmed.

Vesela turned back to her East German colleagues. "They are of no interest to you, gentlemen. They are Bulgarian nationals," she told them.

Rather than hand the papers back to the driver, Vesela walked around the front of the cab to the other door. She indicated to

Tsvetan that he should wind the window down. She handed his and Tatyana's false papers through the window to him.

"May your God go with you," she said and with a sweep of her arm she ordered the guard to raise the barrier.

Ten minutes later Martinov arrived at the border checkpoint. He was exactly ten minutes too late.

Chapter Thirty Five

9 November 1989

Throughout Italy and across Europe everyone was glued to their televisions. Ettore and his wife Bogdana were watching as Radiotelevisione Italiana announced the fall of the Berlin Wall over images of the wall being ripped down by citizens from both sides.

"The Berlin Wall has been breached after nearly three decades keeping East and West Berliners apart. At midnight East Germany's Communist rulers gave permission for gates along the Wall to be opened after hundreds of people converged on crossing points. The East Berliners surged through cheering and shouting and were met by jubilant West Berliners on the other side. Ecstatic crowds immediately began to clamber on top of the Wall and hack large chunks out of the 45-kilometre barrier.

It had been erected in 1961 to stop people leaving for West Germany. From 1949 until the wall went up about two and a half million people had fled East Germany. After 1961, the Wall and other fortifications along the border shared by East and West Germany kept most East Germans in. Many of those attempting to escape have been shot dead by border guards.

The first indication that change was imminent came earlier today when a Communist party spokesman announced East Germans would be allowed to travel directly to West Germany. West German Chancellor Helmut Kohl has hailed the decision to open the Wall as 'historic' and called for a meeting with his East German counterpart."

"I can't believe it, Ettore. Is the nightmare finally coming to the end?" Tears were running down Bogdana's face as she watched, her mouth hanging open in disbelief. "I must ring Mama and Papa. What if they haven't seen the news?"

Ettore looked at his wife in disbelief. "Of course they have seen it. The whole world is watching. Besides, since Hungary and Czechoslovakia opened their borders your father has been watching every news bulletin he can feast his eyes on. Take my word for it, Bogdana. They know."

Bogdana had already started to dial the number. "I must ring them anyway. I want to hear their happiness."

"Hello."

"Mama, it is me. Have you heard the news?"

"Of course. Your father is glued to the television with tears in his eyes. It is only a matter of time, Bogdana. Bulgaria will follow. It is all over."

Bogdana could feel her own tears welling up again and her voice breaking. "I am so happy for you both, and for me. At last I will be able to see my own country."

Her mother's reply was swift. "This is your country, Bogdana. You were born here. Italy has been good to you, to all of us."

"I know that, Mama, but in my heart I am a Bulgarian. I long to go there."

On the other end of the phone her mother was smiling. She was always quick to remind her daughter what they owed the Italian people, but deep down she was glad that Bogdana thought of Bulgaria this way.

"Well, soon you should get your chance," she said. "Your stupidly sentimental father is determined to go back as soon as travel is made possible, although God knows how we will afford it on his teacher's pension."

Bogdana was getting excited, although at that moment Bulgaria was still a closed Communist state. "Next summer in the school holidays we will all go, including Ettore and the children. It will be wonderful," she said.

"Poor Ettore, he probably had a week in Spain or Portugal in mind, not a trip to a grey Communist outpost like Bulgaria," her mother replied.

At this point Tsvetan, who despite being 'glued' to the TV had been listening to their conversation, came over and demanded the phone. Tatyana handed it to him aware that between them her daughter and her husband would come up with some romantic proposal to visit Bulgaria, leaving her and the uncomplaining Ettore to attend to the details.

"Take no notice of your mother, Bulgaria is the most beautiful country on Earth. Why would Ettore want to go to Portugal or Spain when Bulgaria has the best beaches in Europe?"

Bogdana laughed. Between her parents reality got twisted in the most delightful way. "Ettore has no plans to go to those places, Papa. It was just Mama's notion."

Tsvetan was relieved. "Well, I am glad he has seen sense." he announced. "In summer we are going home, all of us."

Chapter Thirty Six

August 1990

A week earlier Tsvetan had celebrated his seventieth birthday. This trip with his family was his present to himself. However, he now thought it would have been better if he and Tatyana had travelled alone.

For his two grandchildren it was their first flight and exciting for that reason. For his son in law Ettore it was a great curiosity. His daughter who had no first-hand experience to prepare her for the trip was bubbling over with anticipation of her first visit to her 'homeland'. Tsvetan and Tatyana felt very differently. Their overwhelming emotion was fear. They were fugitives of the Communist state and although there had been free elections in June the same party, under a different name, was in power.

As the plane prepared for landing at Sofia airport Tatyana gripped Tsvetan's arm so tightly her nails drew blood. Despite this Tsvetan did not pull his arm away.

"We are being silly, Tanya. It was forty years ago and we are Italian citizens. We are totally safe."

Tatyana rested her head on his shoulder and slightly loosened her grip on his arm. "I know, we are being silly, but the greatest moment of relief I have ever experienced in my life was the moment we left this country and here we are voluntarily returning at the first opportunity. You have to admit it feels strange."

Tsvetan nodded. "I know it is strange, but it is our country. For the first time in decades the nation belongs to the people again. We needed to come. We have friends and family to mourn and ghosts to lay to rest. I also pray that I will find my little brother, and most of all that I will find Dido alive."

"Tsvetan, you must not expect to find him. We have talked about this so often. Terrible as it is to think about, Dido probably did not survive that day."

Tsvetan was still after all this time wrestling with the guilt of losing friends so that he could live. He could still conjure up the unwelcome image of Milen's body lying on the shore.

"I know it is improbable, but I have to hope," he told her.

Tatyana snuggled into him under the watchful eye of her daughter across the aisle. "Yes, we have to hope," she replied, her voice trailing off until it was barely audible.

Sofia held no particular memories for Tsvetan, but Tatyana wanted to visit the house where she had lived with her mother and Cleto.

"I know it was an unexceptional house, but it was my last home in Bulgaria. If we are going to try and rekindle some memories from that time then it will help me orientate myself," she told Tsvetan as they sat outside a coffee house in the grey and dusty city centre. "You don't need to come. I am happy to go on my own."

At once Bogdana interjected. "I will come with you, Mama. I want to see everything."

Tatyana placed her hand on her daughter's arm and squeezed it gently. "I would like that," she replied.

Ettore indicated that he was happy to stay with Tsvetan and the children. "We can go and look at the cathedral and according to my guide the parliament building is nearby too," he said, looking at Tsvetan for confirmation.

Bogdana bent and kissed her children and taking her mother's arm set off to see the first landmark in what she regarded as her own history.

The house was larger than Tatyana remembered it, but it was also a little neglected with paint flaking off the walls and the garden, which she remembered with fondness, now sadly overgrown.

"Come on, Mama, we will knock and say who you are," her daughter insisted.

"No, I can't. My mother would have died years ago. I don't want to see strangers in there. It will just upset me."

Bogdana was not for turning. "I will knock," she said and before her mother could object she was striding up to the front door.

Less than five minutes later she was back at her mother's side. "There is nobody there." she reported. "They must be out. We can come back."

This time Tatyana was going to get her way. She was adamant that she was going to leave it at that. Just as she was trying to explain herself to her disappointed daughter she realised that Bogdana was not listening, but was looking at someone approaching from behind her. The old man studied the young woman who was returning his gaze. He could see Tatyana in the face of her daughter and for a moment the years fell away.

"Bella Mia?" he ventured.

Tatyana turned at the sound of her pet name and found herself face to face with Cleto. She ran to him and he scooped her up into his arms while her daughter looked on in wonder. Tatyana had felt afraid, afraid to come to Bulgaria, afraid to think that Cleto, ten years younger than her mother could be alive. Now all fear was gone as she felt the safety that comes from being with someone who loves you unconditionally.

*

In the end they had really enjoyed the trip. Tsvetan and Tatyana had felt immense pride in showing their family what a beautiful country Bulgaria was. Their daughter shared in that pride now refusing to accept she was ever an Italian. Cleto had accompanied them for a large part of the time and he had developed a wonderful bond with Bogdana who revelled in at last having a "nonno" all to herself.

In three days' time they were flying back to Italy and they were still to visit their home town, Svishtov. Tsvetan knew he had been putting it off, unsure how the bittersweet memories would unravel, but it had to be done. At his insistence he and Tatyana were to go there alone with the rest of the family following on a day later. They caught a bus from Veliko Tarnovo where they had been staying and in just one and a half hours the bus turned into the familiar old square. They were home.

Each of them had spent their life wondering about the fate of the other. When they finally met and had their question answered they shook hands and embraced awkwardly. It was not a moment of rapturous joy. For Tsvetan the guilt that he had carried for forty years dissolved away. For Dido it was a box ticked, the final piece of the jigsaw at last found. The two men took a boat ride together and looked over at the island that had shaped their lives. The beautiful banks of Belene Island, radiant in the late summer sunshine, gave no hint of its dark past.

If you enjoyed *Belene Island*, please leave a review on Amazon. Go to https://www.amazon.co.uk/Belene-Island-Geoff-Hart/dp/1980583501

You may also want to read my other books on Amazon, *Bulgaria: Unfinished Business, Second Time Lucky* and *The Icon of Arbanasi.*

Printed in Great Britain
by Amazon

26414460R00118